UNDERCOVER GiRl

#4...Danger

In a world of secrets, how can you
tell what's real?

UNDERCOVER GIRL

UNDERCOVER GIRL

#4...Danger

by Christine Harris

scholastic inc.

New York   Toronto   London   Auckland   Sydney
Mexico City   New Delhi   Hong Kong   Buenos Aires

ISBN 0-439-76128-X

All rights reserved. Published by Scholastic Inc., 557 Broadway, New York, NY 10012, by arrangement with Omnibus Books, an imprint of Scholastic Australia.

12 11 10 9 8 7 6 5 4 3 2 1   6 7 8 9 10 11/0

Printed in the U.S.A.

First American edition, March 2006

b1637731X

UNDERCOVER GIRL

#4...DANGER

1.

Something was seriously wrong.

Jesse stared at Liam, her C2 partner. The color had drained from his face. His skin looked like wax. He jammed his cell phone into his top pocket, turned the ignition key, and gunned the engine. The car shot forward.

Jesse's head thumped back against the headrest. She looked down to check that her seat belt was fastened.

In seconds the car was doing the speed limit, then zoomed past it. Liam always said that the rust patches and dented bumper of his car hid a super motor.

He didn't lie, thought Jesse. *He lies about nearly everything else. But not the car.*

"Where are we going?" Jesse grabbed the bar above the door to steady herself. "I know our C2 assignments are top secret. But if I'm going to die, I'd like to know now."

Liam slammed the car around a corner. A pedestrian leaped on to the sidewalk, shaking his fist.

Liam's shoulders were hunched, his eyes narrowed. "I'm going to pull over and let you out, Jesse. You can't be involved in this."

Her jaw dropped. This was a first. He hadn't shown this much concern on their last assignment when they were stealing dead bodies. "Why? Did Director Granger tell you to do that?"

Liam was silent.

So Granger didn't give that order. "I'm staying," she said.

"This is serious, Jesse." Liam weaved in and out of traffic lanes like a madman. "There are no other agents close by and we only have ten minutes."

Jesse flinched as Liam ran a red light. Other drivers braked suddenly in terror and confusion. "Then you don't have time to drop me off. Every second counts. Besides, I won't let you go into a dangerous situation on your own. It's against the rules."

Liam snorted. "What do you care about rules?"

He was right. If she heard a rule, she was tempted to break it. "I'm a kid. I'm supposed to hate rules." She took a deep breath. "Anyway, I owe you from our last assignment. And you might need two people. Where are we going?"

"The subway. I've never heard that tone in Granger's voice. I think . . . I think he was frightened." Liam's voice trailed into a whisper as though he couldn't believe his own words.

Hot pins and needles shot across Jesse's neck. It was her warning sign, and it was always correct. Director Granger was an "ice man." Cold and ruthless, he rarely revealed emotion. If Liam was right, and Granger was frightened, then something dreadful was about to happen.

Liam wiped perspiration from his top lip with his sleeve. "C2 just had a call from someone who says he's planted a bomb in the subway, at Central Station. Not just an ordinary bomb. It contains anthrax."

2.

No wonder Granger sounded scared.

Jesse knew what happened if someone breathed in anthrax — fever, headache, cough, shortness of breath, and bleeding. There was a ninety percent chance an infected person would die.

Again, she wished she didn't have an extraordinary memory. The details about anthrax were etched in her brain the moment she'd read them.

The car thumped over a strip of shredded truck tire. Jesse bounced high in her seat. She thought of her parents. They had both been killed in a car crash when she was one year old. Nervously, she fingered her seat belt again.

"Are they evacuating the train station?" she asked.

"No."

She looked at him in amazement. "Why not?"

"No time. Not enough warning. We can't evacuate a whole station in ten minutes. And think of the panic. People would trample each other, break bones, fall down the stairs. There might even be deaths."

"We don't have to tell them *why* they have to get out."

"Whatever happens, they can't get out in time."

Jesse still thought they should try. Although she knew that anthrax spores could float for miles. In the 1940s, on a Scottish island, experiments with anthrax meant that no one could live there for fifty years afterward.

"Besides, if there were hundreds of people pushing to get out, how could we reach the bomb?" Liam added.

Privately, she was relieved that C2 hadn't ordered the station to be sealed off, leaving the commuters trapped inside. But that would draw public attention in a huge way. And Director Granger obviously didn't want that.

"Could it be a hoax?"

"Sure. But I don't think so. Granger sounded certain. Still want to come with me?"

"Yes. You never know, you might need a genius." She spoke flippantly, but her excellent memory and ability to think quickly had helped before. "Do the police know about the danger?"

Liam shook his head. "The caller said he'd only contacted C2."

"Do you know where he put the bomb?"

"In a ventilation shaft in the main waiting area."

Jesse groaned. *Not another shaft.* Enclosed spaces made her feel sick. Yet she often ended up crawling into them.

"What do we do if we find this bomb?" she asked.

Liam didn't answer.

Oh great. He doesn't have a plan. Again.

The upper level of Central Station loomed

large in front of them. Liam drove straight for it. The exhaust pipe scraped as he drove over the curb and braked hard.

People on the sidewalk looked startled. A man shouted.

Immediately, Jesse and Liam leaped from the car. Liam didn't stop to close his door. It hung open like an outstretched arm.

As Jesse raced down the concrete ramp, faces blurred. Voices mingled into one raucous noise.

A picture of Rohan and Jai, her C2 "brothers," flashed into her mind. *Will I ever see them again?*

3.

Jesse stopped in the middle of the station waiting area, panting hard from her mad dash. Like Liam, she ignored the curious stares and irritation from people they had pushed aside. She didn't have time to explain.

Peering upward, she spun around in a full circle. "There's a dozen ventilation shafts. Which one is it?"

Liam said a word that probably wasn't in a respectable dictionary.

"Did the caller say anything else about the position of the bomb?" asked Jesse.

"Just what I've told you. No . . . hang on. He said, 'Revenge is sweet.'"

What does that mean? If this guy's crazy enough to plant an anthrax bomb in a crowded station, he could mean anything. Or nothing.

She stepped onto a bench seat to see over the heads of commuters. An idea shot through her like a spear. "Liam! This way." *I might be wrong, but neither of us has a better idea.*

She headed straight for a stand that sold chocolates and candy. Directly above it was a ventilation shaft. "Maybe the guy was making a pun about this candy stand."

He nodded. "Let's try."

She scrambled onto the counter.

The owner, red in the face, stepped forward. "What are you doing?"

"Go away," shouted Liam.

Startled, the man backed off.

Jesse took out her pocket knife, then reached up to the shaft cover. "I'm too short, Liam."

Liam leaped up beside her, grabbed her legs, and hoisted her higher. He wobbled once, then steadied.

Moving quickly despite shaking fingers, she undid the screws of the shaft cover with the knife. The cover dropped with a clatter.

Not far inside was a large box of chocolates. Nothing else was visible. *This must be it.*

She reached inside and gently picked up the box. Instinctively, her eyes half-closed in case it exploded.

Liam wobbled again.

"Don't drop me!"

If she fell now, there was no hope for any of them.

The owner retreated further. "I've called the police."

Jesse ignored him. "Put me down. I've got it." She aimed a questioning look at Liam. "Tell me you know how to disarm this."

He shook his head.

Those ten minutes were almost gone. Desperately, she looked around. Thousands of people were about to die — including herself. There wouldn't be much left of her if it exploded while she was holding it.

Arms out, holding the box carefully in front of her, she sank to the counter, dangled her legs over the side, then dropped to the floor.

If I can get it into one room and shut the

door, then maybe the danger will be contained. Maybe not. But I have to try. Where would I find a room like that?

Liam reached for the box.

Jesse shook her head. "I've got an idea. Clear a path. I'm taking this across to that bathroom."

Without arguing, he pushed a path through the crowd.

A man in a wheelchair was in the doorway of the bathroom.

"Out of the way, please," yelled Jesse.

He frowned. "But I'm disabled."

"Sorry." Liam grabbed the handles on the back of the man's chair and pulled it clear.

"Hey. I've got a certificate that says I can use these facilities before anyone else."

I've got a bomb. I win.

Jesse moved swiftly but smoothly into the room and kicked the door shut behind her.

The lid of the chocolate box popped up and fine powder sprayed over her.

4.

"You're going to push your nose through to the back of your head if you keep rubbing it like that." Jesse sat on a chair in the infirmary isolation room, watching Liam.

"Did Ari have to poke that swab so far up my nostrils?"

Probably not. But I think he enjoyed it.

"He had to find out if we breathed in the powder. Neither of us has any cuts or scratches, so we're OK there."

Liam winced and shifted uncomfortably.

"They steal their antibiotic needles from horses," she said.

"It certainly feels that way. How many

times have you been in this part of the C2 building?"

Jesse shrugged. She didn't want to talk about it. Not now. Not ever. The experiments, the needles, the fear — they were all private, and the memories were locked away, not to be shared. *Rohan's out of the infirmary and I'm in. We're taking turns.*

She stared at the heavy plastic curtain that hung around them, cutting them off from contact with anyone else. Anthrax couldn't be passed from person to person. You had to touch it or breathe it in to become infected. But C2 was taking no chances. She and Liam had been bundled into the mobile hazard van, hosed down, and scrubbed with brushes. Back at C2 they were put in isolation, jabbed with needles, poked, and prodded. But it might all be for nothing. Jesse knew she had breathed in the powder.

She wondered if Granger had issued a public health warning.

"At least it wasn't a real bomb," she said to Liam, in an effort to be positive.

"No. It was spring-loaded to release the

powder. Although if it had remained in that ventilation shaft, the airflow would have spread it. And so would train movements."

"So you owe *me* now."

Liam sighed. "For a thumb sucker, you drive a hard bargain."

"I've told you before, I don't suck my thumb. Ruins the arch of your teeth."

They both fell silent.

Jesse wondered which symptom would come first. Headache, fever? C2's newest medical scientist, Ari, said the nanotechnology used to release a chemical to stimulate her brain and make her a genius might not protect her against anthrax. "I have no experience with this," he had said. Nanites had helped her before, but the virus she had encountered previously attacked the brain. This involved lungs. All those miniature computer-programmed submarines in her head might be useless against anthrax.

All they could do was wait.

5.

Jesse and Liam sat in Granger's office.

A warm feeling spread through her. *I'm alive!* The thought kept looping through her mind as though she'd never realized it before.

Granger smoothed his striped silk tie with one manicured hand. "As you now know, the powder was a simulant. It looks like anthrax, acts like it, but it isn't infectious."

Liam sat forward. "Then what was this all about? If it was a joke, it wasn't funny."

The Director pressed his pale fingers together. A secretive expression flitted across his face, as though he was suppressing what he really wanted to say. "There could be several motives. Perhaps it was a warning. Someone could be telling us, 'Look what I can do.' If they can produce a simulant, they probably have real anthrax spores."

"Have they made any demands?" asked Liam.

"Not yet."

Jesse thought of lions. When they were after prey, they roared loudly. The herd they stalked became so terrified, it scattered. Just what the lions wanted. Then they could pick off their victims one at a time.

"Maybe the people who hid the chocolate box wanted to frighten us," she said. "Isn't that what terrorism is about? It's frightening to have an enemy who darts out of hiding, does damage, then disappears. You don't know when or how they're going to attack. So you're always looking for it."

"Sounds like Nimbus," said Liam.

Granger nodded. "It's possible. That's how they operate. In secret, upsetting order and confidence. They want to break down society into little pieces that won't stick together. Blow this up, kill those, infect them. If they're successful enough, people will start shooting at their own shadows . . . and each other. It's an attack from inside rather than outside."

Jesse had already tangled with the Nimbus organization. They had advanced technology. And they were ruthless.

"An enemy that believes it's right is much harder to fight than one that simply obeys orders."

Jesse watched Granger closely. *What's he thinking that he's not saying?*

"We've fed a story to the media about a report of a chemical leak at the station, which turned out to be a false alarm. Commuters suffered nothing worse than disrupted schedules."

Jesse wondered what Granger would have done if there had been real anthrax. People would have become sick — and died. He couldn't have covered that up.

"The caller could be toying with C2," said Liam. "Whoever it was knew the number to call, and it's not as though it's listed in the phone book."

Granger shrugged.

Jesse was intrigued. This was a gesture that she wouldn't normally associate with

Granger. Shrugging seemed so casual, almost sloppy. Granger was formal and dressed only in designer-label clothing.

"Did you recognize the voice?" asked Liam.

"No." Granger answered far too quickly. "The caller used voice-altering equipment. I can't even be sure if it was a man or a woman." He sighed. "Liam. Ask your sources. Find out if there are whispers about Nimbus. Are they more active lately? What's going on? It's time we tracked down exactly where this group is and cleaned them out."

Jesse shivered. When Granger sent in *cleaners,* it wasn't the sort with mops and brooms.

"Liam, be subtle," said Granger. "We don't want Nimbus to hear we're asking questions."

"I can do subtle."

Granger raised one eyebrow as though he had just heard the mother of all lies. "You're excused, Liam. Jesse, please stay."

Uh-oh. This can't be good.

Liam glanced sideways at her as he passed, but said nothing.

Granger waited till Liam had closed the

door. Then he said, "I have a special task for you, Jesse. One that requires absolute discretion. Fingerprints found on the box were in the employee database. They belong to a man who once worked for our government. I want you to find out if he's involved. Either with Nimbus, or working alone. I want to know if you sense anything suspicious."

"OK."

"This man is old and retired, but he'll sniff out the usual agent a mile away. A child would have more of a chance of getting close to him. Tell no one. Report directly to me. Verbal only. Do not write anything down. Understood?"

Jesse nodded, but she felt uncomfortable. Was Granger suggesting the government had threatened to infect its own people? She knew that it had experimented on unsuspecting citizens before, with anthrax, Q fever, and even radioactive materials. But why use fake anthrax? And why give a warning? Were they testing C2, or was this something personal — a challenge to Director Granger?

Whatever the answer, Jesse was sure

that Granger was keeping information from her. It was like walking blindfolded through a minefield. She couldn't stand still and do nothing. Yet moving forward was filled with danger.

6.

Outside Rohan's door, Jesse took a deep breath to steady the butterflies in her stomach.

Rohan and Jai, her C2 brothers, were part of her earliest memories. They had played games, argued, and told silly jokes to keep away the shadows of fear.

But Rohan had changed.

Two months ago he had disappeared.

"He's dead," Granger had told her. "Forget about him."

As if. She'd continued searching. But when she found Rohan, he was a mess. His face was dreadfully thin. He could no longer walk.

And he'd plucked out every one of his eyelashes.

The only good thing about his disappearance was that Rohan had found his brother.
A real, flesh-and-blood brother, who had the
same parents. That was a surprise. Now they
were separated again. And C2 must never
know there had been contact between the
two boys.

Please don't hate me, Rohan.

Before Jesse could knock, the door opened.
Mary Holt, their carer, stood in the doorway.
Hair frizzy, eyes wide, she gasped. "Jesse.
You startled me. What are you doing?"

"Nothing."

"Then go and do nothing somewhere else."

"I mean, nothing that I'm not supposed to
do. I came to see Rohan."

Mary glanced over her shoulder into the
room behind her. "He's a little tired today.
Aren't you, dear?"

The old Rohan would have loathed being
called "dear," especially by Mary. He said
people used terms like that when they couldn't
remember your name, or didn't want to
use it.

But this Rohan was silent. About every-thing.

Jesse simply smiled. "I won't stay long."

Mary was like a snake — all right as long as you didn't provoke her. But watch out if you did. She had a long memory and the power to schedule extra hours in the gymnasium or the laboratory.

"Make sure you keep your word." Mary loped off along the corridor.

Jesse entered Rohan's room and closed the door.

He sat in an armchair, facing a wall.

"Hi, Rohan," said Jesse in a cheerful voice.

He didn't look up.

She took a small device from her pocket and scanned the room for listening devices. Mary had been in here for a reason. And it wasn't because she wanted to be a nurse. C2 would keep a close eye on Rohan. For a short time, he had escaped. That would make them nervous.

It must be torture being back here, thought Jesse. *And it's my fault.*

7.

Jesse found a small listening device, the size of a lentil, tucked under the bedside table. Deftly, she picked it off, took it into the bathroom, and flushed it down the toilet. *Hate to think what sounds you'll pick up down there.*

She, Jai, and Rohan always destroyed any eavesdropping equipment they found in their rooms, but neither Mary nor anyone else at C2 ever mentioned it. That would be admitting that they were spying on the children from Operation IQ. C2 seethed with secrets. This was just another.

Jesse grabbed a chair and placed it

directly in front of Rohan. He stared at a point somewhere over her right shoulder.

I never wanted to hurt you, she thought, then asked aloud how he was feeling.

"Better."

She smothered a sigh. *This is as hard as checking a hen's mouth for teeth. And they don't have any.*

"I have a joke for you," she said. "Why do bees hum?"

Rohan said nothing.

"Because they can't sing!" *Is that a smile?*

"Jai will be here soon," she added. At nine, he was the youngest of the three, and continually nervous. Rohan's disappearance had upset him more than he admitted.

"Did Ari explain to you about replacing the faulty nanites we have in our bodies, and how they work to make us smarter?"

Rohan nodded.

"He told you that we need to have the chemical the nanites release or we'll die? Did you understand it all?"

He raised one eyebrow.

Now that's more like the old Rohan. He would never admit it if he didn't know something. He'd make up an answer, which made it difficult to work out when he really *did* know.

Since his return, his wall of silence had stopped her talking about anything important. But not anymore.

"Something happened today," she said. "I . . . I thought I was going to die."

He blinked. Without eyelashes, his eyes reminded her of a lizard's.

"I can't tell you what happened," she said, "but I was worried that I wouldn't have a chance to explain or say I was sorry."

"Don't say sorry."

Whoopee. Three words, all together. That was the longest sentence he'd completed since his return.

"I know you hate it here. How much you wanted to escape. And I spoiled it for you. Now you're back and you're a . . ." She swallowed the word *prisoner.* "You're stuck here again. I feel really bad. But you were dying. Your body and mind were breaking down.

You couldn't walk. Your words didn't make sense."

Rohan looked aside.

Jesse remembered her relief at finding Rohan hidden in the dilapidated shed, then her agony in deciding that the only way to save his life was to bring him back to C2 headquarters. "You were ill. What was I supposed to do? Leave you to die?"

"Yes."

That word hit her like a slap on the face. "I promise the three of us will find a way to be free. There's a lot to tell you, about other Operation IQ geniuses, all kinds of things." She swallowed hard. "I missed you so much while you were away. I was really happy when I found you. Don't hate me for bringing you back."

Rohan looked at her then, and slowly shook his head. "I don't hate you. I hate me."

She stared back at him. "Why?"

"Because I let you down. You and Jai." His bottom lip trembled. "You wouldn't do that. I was the computer whiz. Jai breathes his music. But you . . . you're the strong one."

"You remember what happened?"

"Everyone thinks I lost my memory when the nanites malfunctioned. But I didn't. It was my first field assignment," said Rohan. "I was outside, by myself. I . . . the sun was shining and it was exciting, so I ran away and left you and Jai behind. Then it was too late to come back. C2 would have punished me. I thought I might not be allowed outside ever again. Then I became ill."

"It doesn't matter now," she said. "Forget it. I'm not going to let go of my brother because he made a mistake. We're not superheroes. We're just kids. OK. We're smart. And kind of good-looking . . ."

This time she was sure he smiled.

Yet her own smile hid a knot of worry. The danger was not over yet. C2 might not forget so easily.

8.

Jesse ran full speed along the hallway of the apartment building. Her shoes thumped on the tiled floor, echoing in the stairwell.

She stopped at apartment 503.

Frantically, she banged on the door with her fist. "Is anyone there? Help!"

She heard the rumble of a deep voice, then the sliding of a heavy bolt. The door opened a fraction. One pale blue eye protected by a shaggy white eyebrow peered out at her across a door chain.

"A man's following me. I . . ." Jesse pointed to a sticker. "This is a Safety House. Please let me in." She threw a terrified glance over her shoulder.

He pushed the door shut again. Then Jesse heard the rattle of a chain being moved.

The door swung wide open.

A tall, elderly man with white hair beckoned. "Come in."

Jesse shot inside.

"Wait here. Don't let anyone in but me." The old man grabbed a baseball bat that was propped against the wall. He stepped outside and closed the door behind him.

I bet that baseball bat isn't for sport. Jesse directed a keen look around the room. Her first impression was color. There were shelves so overloaded with books that they sagged in the middle. The sofa was decorated with red cushions. And there were huge leafy potted plants, some with flowers. Three framed prints of propeller planes in flight hung on the walls.

A knock came at the door.

She stepped forward and peered through the spy hole. *It's him.* She opened the door and let the old man back in.

"No one around. You must have frightened him off with all your noise." He replaced the bat, then slid the bolt and chain back into place.

Jesse noticed his hands. Although they were marked with brown age spots, his skin looked soft and the nails were clean.

"Are you aware, young lady, that any noise over eighty-five decibels damages hearing?"

She knew that, but she simply shook her head. "Do you keep that baseball bat for the kids who come here looking for a Safety House?"

He fluffed his top lip with air. "All these years and you're my first rescue. I'd forgotten about the sign." He looked her up and down. "Did that man hurt you?"

She knew he would see a nervous girl — with short brown hair and a smattering of freckles — clutching a shoulder bag.

"No. I just . . . got scared," she said. "And everywhere I went, there he was. Right behind me."

The old man frowned. "Sounds familiar."

It does? Do they have a regular stalker in this apartment building?

"What are we going to do with you?" he asked.

"May I have a drink, please?" She softened her voice, made it sound hesitant. Before he could refuse, she sat on the sofa and put her head in her hands. "My parents are both working. There's no one home. And I'm scared to be alone." Jesse heard her own voice and wanted to slap herself for whining. But she had to find out more about the old man.

"Of course. Where are my manners? I can make you a tasty herbal infusion. Perk you up a bit. I'll cut some fresh leaves. Want to see my garden?"

This should be interesting. He lives five floors up.

"We haven't introduced ourselves. I'm Walter Preston."

"I'm Miranda," said Jesse.

"Call me Walter."

Movement in the inner doorway drew Jesse's attention. Adrenaline rushed through her body. A boy about her own age stood there, holding a large knife with both hands.

9.

Jesse remained absolutely still, not taking her eyes off the boy.

"Daniel," said Walter Preston in a firm voice. "We have a visitor. Put down the knife."

The boy retreated silently into the room behind him.

Walter shrugged. "His aunt lives in a nearby apartment. He stays here quite a bit. Gets bored at home alone. He's helping me chop herbs today."

Chop? With a knife that big it would be more like mash.

Walter kept a baseball bat behind the door and his young friend clutched a large knife.

Being secluded in C2 meant that Jesse some-times had trouble deciding what was normal. But this time she had no doubt. *These two are weird.*

Walter put one hand to his head.

"Are you all right?" asked Jesse.

"Yes, just a headache. I didn't sleep well last night." He forced a smile, which didn't reach his eyes. "Oh well, one day I'll begin sleeping for a long time, so I'll catch up then."

Was he sick? He certainly sounded depressed. A man who thought he was dying would have nothing to lose. He might not be afraid of the consequences of what he did.

"Come on." Walter gestured for Jesse to follow. "Let's go into the garden."

They entered a large kitchen. There was a row of blue canisters along one bench. Bunches of herbs tied with string hung from a wall shelf. The room was sparkling clean and smelled of spicy disinfectant and some kind of lemon herb.

Daniel stood in front of a wooden chop-ping board. A bundle of half-chopped leaves sat in the middle of it. He still held a knife, but this time it was a smaller version.

"Daniel, meet . . ." Walter hesitated.

"Miranda," said Jesse.

Daniel nodded. His skin was pale. It made his dark brown eyes stand out. Daniel had beautiful eyes, but there was something odd about them.

Jesse thought of another child who had crossed her path. One who came from Nimbus. That girl was genetically engineered to have no feelings, so that she could kill without guilt. Jesse knew there were other genetically altered children out there, trained to follow Nimbus's orders.

"The garden's out here," said Walter, beckoning. He slid a large bolt on a door on the other side of the kitchen. Then he turned the lock.

His apartment was cozy and attractive, but it wasn't a mansion full of art treasures that would attract burglars. So why all the locks?

"Do you want me to put on the tea kettle?" asked Daniel. His words were polite, but he directed a hard stare in Jesse's direction.

Walter smiled warmly. "Thanks, my boy. Much appreciated."

The door led out on to a balcony.

Walter paused, with Jesse directly behind him. He took a pair of glasses from his top pocket and slipped them on. Then he looked left, right, and across at the windows of the next-door apartment building.

Jesse knew he was checking for something — or some*one*. But they were five floors aboveground.

Then Walter relaxed. "I have a hundred pots out here."

Jesse was impressed with his balcony garden. The plants were green and luxuriant. His pots, artistically arranged, were in a variety of bold colors.

Walter's glasses slipped down the bridge of his nose as he bent to check a plant. He mumbled something Jesse didn't catch.

She listened more carefully.

"The mint. Parsley . . ." Walter pressed his lips together as though he were restraining anger.

Jesse tried to see what was upsetting him, but failed. Maybe he saw bugs or wilted leaves.

"It was yellow. Yellow." He turned his

head and bellowed. "Daniel. What color is the parsley pot?"

"Yellow," called Daniel from the kitchen.

"I knew it."

"See, it's orange." Walter glared at Jesse.

There isn't a lot of difference between yellow and orange.

"Someone's changed the pots."

"Why would they do that?"

He shook his head. "Silly me. I remember now. I changed the pots myself the other day. Slipped my mind."

Jesse didn't believe him. Walter Preston was lying.

10.

Walter picked leaves from several plants. "See this mint? Tradition dictates that it should be planted at midnight. And the parsley? Well, it's said that only a wicked person can grow it successfully."

It was only a superstition. Yet Jesse noticed his parsley spilled over the sides of the pot.

He touched a plant with grayish-blue leaves. "If you make an infusion with this sage and green tea leaves, then rinse your hair in it, it restores natural color in someone who's going gray." He chuckled. "Too late for me."

Walter's hair was totally white.

He was gentle with the plants, handling the leaves tenderly. Jesse tried to imagine those hands placing a fake bomb in an air-conditioning duct. Could Walter climb up that high? Her eyes swayed toward Daniel in the kitchen. Maybe Walter had an accomplice.

"This one's the best," said Walter. "Chocolate mint."

She caught the aroma the moment his fingers touched the leaves. Jesse's sense of smell was extra-sensitive, thanks to the work of the nanites in her body. They were so small it was impossible to see them. Yet they helped her brain work faster and her eyes see better in the dark. She could also detect the faintest of aromas.

Jesse followed Walter Preston back through the door into the kitchen. He locked the door, then slid the bolt.

Walter put a leaf in each of three blue mugs and filled them with hot water. It smelled delicious.

He put the mugs on the table. "I've got cookies somewhere."

While he rattled jars and rustled packets in a cupboard, Daniel sat opposite Jesse. His skin was blotchy and he sweated as though it was hot. He picked up his mug and gulped greedily at his herbal infusion.

Jesse took a sip of her drink. *Ow.* She touched her top lip. Her eyes watered. *That's hot.* Her tongue felt rough as though someone had scraped it with a scouring pad.

Her eyes swung back to Daniel.

The water was hot. Yet Daniel had swallowed it as though it were only lukewarm.

II.

Abruptly Daniel stood up. "I have to go home now."

Walter spun around. "So soon? You've probably got homework to do, I suppose."

Daniel nodded, then headed into the next room.

Walter followed him. "I'll see you out."

Running away, Daniel? Jesse heard them talking at the front door. She couldn't hear what they said. They spoke too quietly.

She looked up. A light globe, topped by a lime-green shade, dangled above the table. Swiftly, she climbed on her chair and reached up to place a tiny listening device under the shade.

Jesse heard the door bolt slide back into position.

She scrambled back to her seat and sipped at her drink just as Walter came back into the kitchen. "He's what I call a lost soul, that boy."

He's what I call weird.

The phone rang.

Walter's face went as white as his hair. There was a tremor in his right hand.

The phone kept ringing, piercing and insistent.

Uncertainly, Walter threw a look at Jesse, then walked into the living room.

Through the crack of the open door, she watched him hesitate, then pick up the receiver. "Hello?" There was a fresh quaver in his voice. Suddenly he sounded a lot older.

He was silent for a few seconds. When he did speak, his voice was louder, aggressive. "Who is this?" He slammed down the phone.

When Walter returned to the kitchen, Jesse asked innocently, "Wrong number?"

Walter blinked rapidly.

A picture of Daniel's face flicked into her

mind. *That's why his eyes don't look right. He doesn't blink.*

"Yes," said Walter. "Wrong number."

"Do you get a lot of them?" Jesse sipped her chocolate mint infusion.

"Uh . . . yes. My number is close to the one for the pizza place."

"You could buy an answering machine," suggested Jesse. "My parents have one. They listen to the messages when they get home and pick who they want to call back."

Suspicion entered Walter's eyes. "No, I can't have an answering machine. They're not safe. Other people could listen to my conversations."

"Why would anyone do that?"

Walter ran one hand over his face as though he was sandpapering his skin. "I know things. I might be old and retired, but I'm not stupid. They take my newspapers, you know. Sometimes I find them a week later in the wrong place, all placed in a neat bundle."

"Who takes your papers?"

"They've underestimated me. When they

decapitate cockroaches, it's the old ones who run faster from predators."

She imagined cockroaches running around with no heads. *What would it matter if they were fast? They wouldn't run for long if their heads were missing.*

Jesse couldn't figure out what was going on here. Not yet. But one thing was certain — Walter Preston was a frightened man.

12.

Jesse waited in the hallway outside Walter's apartment, listening as he slid home the bolt and chain. He'd locked himself in again.

She took a careful look around. *There don't seem to be security cameras. Good.*

Instead of heading downstairs, she went up to the eighth floor. She walked slowly along the corridor, alert for anything out of place. The building was steeped in aromas: cat food, old trash, fried onions, some sort of cleaning product, even a dose of perfume.

Loud music drifted from 802, voices from 805.

Which apartment belonged to Daniel's aunt? Jesse hoped Daniel wouldn't step out and see her. It might be hard to explain why she was roaming the corridors alone.

A middle-aged woman, shabbily dressed but smiling broadly, passed Jesse in the corridor. "Good afternoon."

Jesse smiled back.

The woman didn't look at her twice. She simply unlocked her door, waited a second for a white cat to prowl around her ankles, then entered an apartment.

On the seventh floor, a man and a woman were arguing. *So he's not taking out the trash and it's his turn. Big deal.* It didn't seem important enough to shout that much. The couple was silly, but not suspicious.

Continuing downstairs, she stopped at apartment 603. It was directly above Walter's. She was still the only one in the corridor. It would be busier later in the day when people returned home from work.

She heard a muffled voice from behind the door. She recognized it instantly. The hairs on her arms stood up.

Ear close to the door, she listened. *No footsteps. No doors opening or closing.* Senses alert for trouble, she knocked firmly on the door.

There was no response.

She took latex gloves from her bag and put them on. Then she selected a small metal instrument. She checked left and right, then inserted the instrument into the lock. It took only a few seconds to jiggle it into the right position. There was a soft click.

Silently, she slipped through the partially open door, remembering to look behind it. She had been surprised before by someone hiding behind an open door, and she wasn't about to let it happen again. This time, there was no one ready to pounce. She closed the door quietly and took stock of her surroundings.

The voices had stopped.

Apartment 603 had a musty smell, as though the windows had not been opened in a while.

There was no sign that anyone else was present, but she checked carefully. No cushions, flowers, or books brightened the apartment. The bed was made, but there were no shoes underneath it and no clothes in the closet. In the bathroom, there was a fresh hand towel and a bar of pink soap. It was set up for someone to live here, yet it didn't have any personal items.

Jesse tried the kitchen. The cupboards held a couple of saucepans, a few stained plates, and mugs. There was a large microwave and an oven. The fridge, although switched on, contained no food. There was the faintest aroma of smoke, as though someone had carried it in on their clothes.

Satisfied that she was alone in the apartment, she headed back to the living room. There was a tape recorder on a side table. She bent to look beneath it. Electrical wires snaked from the machine, down behind the table, and into the floor. That floor was also Walter's ceiling.

Cautiously, she took a pen from her shoulder bag to press REPLAY. Recorded voices began again. "Yes. Wrong number." *That's definitely Walter.*

"Do you get a lot of them?" Jesse gave a small shiver as she heard her own voice.

13.

Jesse exited the building with more questions than answers. *Why set up a recording machine to play back voices in an empty apartment? Because they want someone else to hear it. Who? Walter? That could mean someone's playing nasty tricks on him.*

The scream of an approaching siren cut across her thoughts.

She sniffed the air like a dog catching a scent. *Smoke.*

A fire truck braked and pulled in beside the curb. The siren stopped. Burly men in yellow jackets and hard hats leaped out.

"Around the back, George," shouted one

of the men. "Check it out while we get the hose ready."

Three or four passersby joined Jesse, watching curiously. A curl of smoke rose from behind the building she had just left. Either it wasn't serious or it was just starting.

The firefighter named George jogged around the side of the building and disappeared.

"Stand back, please," called the man who was obviously in charge. "Spectators make our job more difficult."

There were a dozen people in a small group, with several others heading across the street to join them. Jesse edged her way into the middle. She would be better camouflaged if she was surrounded by other people.

George returned. "Ralph. It's just a fire in a recycling bin. I'll grab the garden hose. No need for ours. Maybe you should send someone up to talk to the owner of the bin. Apartment five-oh-three."

Jesse had seen and heard enough. She eased backward through the swelling crowd and moved away.

That's Walter's bin. Had he gone downstairs while she was searching the rest of his building and lit the fire? Or had someone else done it as some kind of message? It sounded like more of a nuisance act than one designed to actually burn down the building.

The hint of smoke she had detected had not been in Walter's apartment. It had been in the one above it.

Uncertainty flooded through her. *I haven't got a clue about what's going on. What am I going to tell the Director?*

14.

Outside Director Granger's office, three levels belowground, Jesse stood still while a light beam scanned her retinas. The panel beneath her feet monitored her heart rate and weight.

"Jesse Sharpe, you are cleared for entry."

That computerized voice was beginning to sound familiar. She could almost believe it belonged to a real person.

In the waiting room, the office manager, Prov, sat behind her desk.

Jesse always looked forward to seeing what she was wearing. She had the most amazing collection of fluffy mohair tops and in-your-face blouses. Jesse doubted Prov had ever worn a pale color in her life. Bright colors suited her strong personality and her huge brown eyes.

Prov smiled. Her teeth were white against her olive skin. "Hello, honey." She beckoned. "The Director said you'd be dropping in this afternoon, so I brought you a treat. Don't tell that woman."

"I never tell her anything." Jesse knew Prov meant Mary Holt. When Prov and Mary were in the same room, there was enough electricity in the air to light up a city block. They were total opposites. *Healthy body, healthy mind,* was Mary's motto. *Sweets for a sweet,* was Prov's. Besides, Mary insulted Prov by calling her *Provincial,* when her full name was actually *Providenza.*

Prov took a chocolate bar from the drawer of her desk and gave it to Jesse.

Mary would go ballistic if she knew. She was fanatical — about everything.

"How's Rohan?" whispered Prov. There were no listening devices in this area. It was scanned each night. The walls were extra thick and built of material that made it impossible to use long-range listening equipment. But a smart person would always be cautious.

"Better. I think he's going to be all right," said Jesse. "It's as though the light's come back on in his eyes."

Prov nodded.

Jesse looked at her curiously. Prov was a soft and fluffy sort of person, yet she had security clearance. She was some kind of C2 agent, and trusted. Otherwise she wouldn't be working this close to the Director, handling his files and seeing who visited him. Yet Jesse could not imagine Prov tailing someone or getting into tae kwon do. It would mess up her hair.

Prov pressed a button on her speaker phone. "Jesse Sharpe is here to see you, sir."

The door to the inner office opened immediately. "Come in." Granger's voice was curt.

He closed the door and sat down at his desk. "Report."

Briefly, she filled him in on the strangeness of Daniel and Walter's fear and his odd behavior. Then she told Granger about the fire in the recycling bin.

He frowned.

"I put one bug into the kitchen light," said Jesse. "But I couldn't get into the other rooms. I'll do that tomorrow."

"I've had receiving equipment put into your room and told Ms. Holt to keep out for now. I don't want anyone else in on this." Granger began fiddling with a pen on his desk.

No Mary Holt! Jesse felt as though a weight had been lifted from her shoulders. If there were any listening devices in her own room, Granger would have to order their removal, or other agents might find out what was being said in Walter's flat.

"You can listen to the tapes in your room. But don't stay up all night. A tired brain is useless."

"Do you have other agents watching Walter Preston?" she asked.

He shook his head.

She didn't think so. Granger had insisted on total secrecy. But she wanted to check. "Then someone else is watching him." Jesse told him about the apartment above Walter's and the recorded conversation. "I didn't take the recorder away. Then they'd know I'd been in there. Whoever *they* are."

She wondered if Walter could have set up that tape recording himself, to make it appear that he was under surveillance when he actually wasn't. But she said nothing. It would only arouse more questions for which she had no answers. And she had no proof.

"You suspect this boy, Daniel, is eaves-dropping on Preston's apartment?"

She shrugged. "He's there a lot. Walter trusts him. Maybe. I don't know."

"*Don't know* isn't good enough. Find out."

Daniel didn't blink. He drank hot water without feeling pain. Was he one of those genetically engineered Nimbus children? If so, what else could he do? And what was his mission?

15.

Jesse sensed a strange atmosphere the moment she entered Rohan's room. She had come directly from Granger's office and her nerves were still on edge.

Jai and Rohan leaned forward, facing each other, obviously involved in a serious discussion. The room was silent now, but they were still frozen in that position, as though waiting for a photograph to be taken.

At first, the boys might have suspected it was Mary opening the door. But the silence continued after they realized it wasn't. And it went on for too long.

Jai's nervous tic began under one eye.

"What are you two talking about?" asked Jesse.

"Nothing . . . music . . ." They both spoke at once.

"So was it nothing or music?" She slumped into a chair beside Rohan. It had been a long day and she was tired. Too tired to work out the riddle of her C2 brothers' behavior.

"It was both," said Rohan.

"You weren't talking about me, were you?"

Both boys made noises of protest, but neither of them actually said no. They didn't look at each other. Another sure sign that they shared some secret.

Jesse felt a stab of hurt. While Rohan was missing, she had spent hours reassuring Jai. She had risked a lot to search for Rohan. Bringing him back had been complicated. She had drawn Liam into her plan, which also put him in danger. If anyone found out that they had tricked Granger into restoring Rohan, they would all be in trouble. And now she was holding the knowledge that Rohan had not lost his memory when his nanites broke down. He had run away. If Granger knew . . . Jesse didn't want to imagine what he would do.

Yet here were Rohan and Jai, shutting her out. A familiar sense of loneliness wrapped around her.

Rohan looked at Jesse's face. "I'm sorry, Jesse. We *were* talking about something."

"That's OK," she said. "You don't have to tell me. I can't tell you about what *I* was doing today."

"That's different. That's work. We were talking about something personal," said Rohan. "We weren't sure how you would . . . if you'd want to know."

Jesse noted that although he was still thinner than he used to be, Rohan's face had filled out. He was obviously healthier. That blank, foggy expression was now replaced by a spark that showed the old Rohan was still around.

"She should be told," said Jai in his careful way. "It is her right. It is important. Besides, we have always been honest with each other about personal things."

Rohan shifted awkwardly.

So he hasn't told Jai he left us behind. I don't blame him.

Jesse smacked her hands together. "This is driving me nuts. Tell me or forget about it altogether."

Rohan sighed. "Do you remember just before I went . . . missing I told you I'd hacked into some C2 files?"

She nodded. At one time, she'd wondered if that was the reason for his disappearance. Sometimes she told herself that he'd been bragging. He exaggerated sometimes. Mostly, she didn't mind. It made him fun to be around. If something was slightly crooked, to Rohan it was mangled. If he had a bruise, his leg was in danger of falling off.

The troubled expression on his face today suggested that, this time, he was not exaggerating. "I couldn't get into everything on the computer system. I didn't have time. And I don't even know if I could have found more anyway. C2 security is tight. But I did find out some things about us. You won't like hearing it."

16.

Early the next morning, Jesse was back at Walter's apartment.

The door swung open suddenly. Jesse jumped. She hadn't expected such a quick response.

Walter's left eyebrow rose. "What are you doing here, Miranda?"

It always took her a moment to adjust when someone called her by a cover name on assignments.

"I brought you this . . . to thank you for looking after me yesterday." She held out a large box of chocolates. It was identical to the one that had been hidden in the subway station.

She studied Walter's expression. He showed no guilt or nervousness. "That's the nicest thing anyone's done for me in a long time, young lady." He took the box and held it awkwardly as though he was deciding whether to put it down or hang on to it. "Why aren't you in school?"

"I have a teacher workshop day and my parents are working." She shrugged.

"Ah, yes. The invisible parents."

He's got that right.

"But you seem to be turning out OK. Being a parent isn't easy. No matter what parents do, children can disappoint them." Sadness came into his eyes.

Jesse felt her heart squeeze in sympathy. *People let you down sometimes.*

She thought back to the previous day. She had seen no family photos in Walter's apartment. Perhaps they were in one of the other rooms.

"Well, thank you again." Walter moved the door a fraction to indicate that he intended to close it.

"Um ... I told my mom about your

chocolate mint and she's never heard of it. Do you think I could take a couple of leaves home? She'd love it." Jesse smiled. "She might even let me off doing the dishes tonight."

Walter fixed his piercing blue eyes on her, then gestured for her to enter. "As a matter of fact, my plant started as a cutting from a friend. Why don't I put a cutting in a pot for your mother? Then she can have her own plant."

"That's great."

"One good turn deserves another. Besides, it's good luck to share a plant."

She followed him into the kitchen. The smell of oregano lingered in the air.

The *clang, bang* of a garbage truck emptying trash cans echoed up from downstairs.

Walter took his glasses from his pocket, put them on, and glared out of the window. His face hardened. "They're at it again." He put both hands over his ears. "All night they've been doing that. There can't be that many trash cans in the whole suburb."

All night? That sounds a bit over the top.

Walter grabbed a brown jacket from the

back of a chair. "Wait here. I'm going down to have a word with them. Lock the door and don't let anyone in."

Garbage collectors seemed harmless compared to axe murderers or terrorists. But Walter obviously had a problem with them.

He stormed out into the hallway. Jesse heard his feet stamping on the stairs as he headed down to ground level.

Jesse locked the door. *Now's my chance.* This room was directly beneath the main room in 603. She took a few steps to her left. *Here!* This would be the place where the wires attached to the recording machine upstairs had disappeared.

She dragged a chair across and climbed onto it. Then she reached up to unclip the top of the smoke alarm. Tucked neatly inside was a bugging device connected to a wire that went up into the ceiling. *That's not part of the smoke alarm.* She tugged at the wire, broke the connection, then replaced the top.

It was clumsy eavesdropping equipment. There were better ways to collect information. Why use old-fashioned wires when you could use detached electronic receivers?

She hopped down and put the chair back where it belonged. *Maybe that's the point. Someone wants Walter to know he's being watched.*

Quietly and efficiently, she scanned his apartment for other listening devices aside from hers. But there were none. *Time for a quick look around.*

Walter didn't have a computer. That was unusual. However, she discovered a lot about him in just a few minutes. He was diabetic. *He won't be eating those chocolates unless he wants to go into a coma.* He was a retired biologist with several degrees. *He's smart.* There were books on germs, viruses, and biological weapons. *He knows about anthrax.*

17.

Jesse found a large scrapbook in the bottom drawer of Walter's desk. It was filled with newspaper and magazine cuttings. She didn't have time to read them all. So she took a camera disguised as lip gloss from her shoulder bag and photographed each page.

She had barely replaced the book when Walter knocked at the door.

"The minute the truck driver saw me, he took off," he said.

Maybe he'd finished emptying the trash cans.

"I was just on my way down to the corner store to buy some milk when you knocked. Feel like a walk?" he asked, the mint forgotten. "I have to get out of here for a while. Sometimes I feel as though these walls are closing in on me."

Jesse understood that feeling.

Walter set off at a swift pace. Jesse had to jog to keep up. He had the advantage of long legs. She had to take two steps for every one of his.

Their progress slowed as he stopped at each corner to peer down side streets. Where there were tall fences, he behaved as though stalkers were lurking behind them. He looked over his shoulder. Any sound distracted him, and there were plenty of those. It was a busy area, with lots of cars.

"How long have you been retired?" asked Jesse.

Walter huffed. "Not long enough. I should have gotten out years ago."

"Where did you work?"

"In a laboratory, as a biologist."

Jesse gave a slight shudder. Bad memories were triggered by that word.

He aimed his blue eyes at her. "You ask a lot of questions."

His eyes reminded her of someone. Who?

Walter looked away and the image changed. *Maybe I was mistaken.*

"My parents tell me that, too." As usual, Jesse felt uncomfortable making up stories about her parents. But what choice did she have? She couldn't say that a secret organization took her in when she was one, turned her into a genius, then sent her out on spy missions. People wouldn't believe it, anyway. If she told a lie about her parents, strangers believed her. If she told the truth, they'd accuse her of lying. Life was all mixed up. What she had learned the night before from Rohan made it seem more muddled than ever.

"You get many answers out of your parents when you ask your questions?" asked Walter.

"Sometimes." She grinned.

Suddenly Walter grasped her wrist with tense fingers.

Jesse balanced lightly on her feet, ready to defend herself. But a small voice at the back of her mind said that if he intended to attack her, he would have done it in the apartment, where there were no witnesses.

"That man on the sidewalk. I've seen him

before," said Walter. "Don't let him catch you looking."

Trying to appear casual and uninterested, Jesse gave the man a quick glance. Shabbily dressed, with ratty hair, he sat with his back propped against a storefront. He draped one protective arm over a large striped bag.

"Maybe this is his spot," she whispered. "He might sleep around here. You probably see him when you go to buy your milk."

"He's watching me," said Walter.

"He's not even looking at us."

"That doesn't mean he's not watching."

Walter had a point. Jesse had been taught to avoid eye contact when she was following someone. *Pretend you're not interested in the target. Act casually. Move slowly. Blend in.*

"There's a battle going on," said Walter. "And I intend to win."

"A battle?"

His bottom lip trembled, then he steadied it. "A battle for the minds of men. Or, in my case, one man." He took a deep breath. "Remember, show no fear."

Walter kept a grip on her arm as they passed the homeless man on the sidewalk.

The man stared vacantly and plucked at his straggly beard.

Jesse looked back over her shoulder.

Director Granger had once shown her a photograph of a man begging her for money in the mall. *You were tagged,* Granger said. *He's one of our agents. In a real situation, you'd be dead.*

Today, the raggedly dressed man paid them no attention. Yet something was wrong. He certainly wore shabby clothes, but they were spotless. There was no dirt embedded around his fingernails or stuck in the wrinkles of his knuckles. The skin on his hands was too smooth for someone living roughly and rummaging through trash looking for food.

Walter was right. That man in the ragged clothes was not who he pretended to be.

18.

Jesse sat at her desk in C2 headquarters with her chin propped in her hands. *How am I supposed to complete this assignment by myself?* There was Walter to keep an eye on, Daniel, the apartment above. She was doing her best, but she couldn't be everywhere at once.

Usually, Granger sent two agents out together. Several times, Jesse had been part of a whole team. But this time, he'd insisted on total secrecy. "No one's to know about this. *No one.*" A worm of doubt wriggled through her. *Is he setting me up? Giving me a job that's impossible for one person to complete so he can say I failed?* She shook her head. It didn't seem logical. But she had been betrayed before. It could happen again.

She sighed. *Keep your brain busy, girl.*

Already, a phone trace for the last month had revealed something strange about Walter's incoming phone calls. They were all from public phones.

Jesse switched on her computer and gave her fingerprints and four passwords.

She swung on her chair while she viewed pictures of the corridor outside apartment 603. Earlier in the day, before visiting Walter, she had inserted a tiny spy camera into the corridor light fixture. It was just as well that the supply department asked no questions. As long as they had authorization from someone superior, they handed over whatever was needed. And there was no one more superior in this organization than the Director.

The spy camera was aimed directly at the entrance to the apartment above Walter's. Tenants walked past, up and back, at different times. A white cat as well. But no one went inside apartment 603.

No clues there.

Next, she inspected the digital images of Walter's scrapbook on her screen.

He had cuttings from around the world about outbreaks of sickness. United States — hantavirus passed on from mice droppings, a smuggled sample of bird flu discovered by customs. Australia — dengue fever from mosquito bites. Britain — the discovery of smallpox virus in a lunchbox that had sat in a refrigerator in a laboratory for forty years. Singapore — an entire apartment block sealed off because of SARS. Russia — a scientist who accidentally pierced his hand with a virus and died horribly. There were hundreds of similar stories.

If half of these stories were true, she understood why Walter had trouble sleeping.

The last cutting was a surprise. It was from a recent newspaper, talking about the mistaken report of a chemical spill in Central Station.

Her shoulders slumped. Walter was eccentric, but she liked him. Maybe that was *why* she liked him. *Please don't be involved, Walter.* It would be so much easier if all the bad guys were ugly and horrible. But they weren't. Sometimes bad people had nice manners or sweet smiles. They had children or pets and told silly jokes. Jesse knew she had to look deeper than that. People were not always who they seemed to be. Rohan's discovery in the C2 computer files had confirmed that.

She slipped on a pair of headphones and listened to the sounds in Walter's apartment. Daniel had visited again.

Walter: "He was there today, outside a store. This time he was trying to look like a homeless man. Miranda saw him."

Daniel: "The same man?"

Walter: "Yes."

Daniel: "What did you do?"

Walter: "Kept walking. I couldn't do anything else. I'm too old to challenge him to a fight. Besides, they'd just send someone else." (There was a sound like that of a cupboard door being closed.)

Daniel: "Do you trust that Miranda?"

Walter: "She's only a girl."

Daniel: "David was only a boy when he killed the giant Goliath with a single stone."

Walter: "If they wanted me dead, I wouldn't be here now. But just in case . . . you know what to do if anything happens to me, don't you?"

19.

Jesse strode along the street, the breeze ruffling her hair. A flurry of people heading for home swirled around her. Lights were gradually coming on. This was her favorite time of day. The grimy city turned into something bright and magical.

She half-expected someone to tap her on the shoulder and drag her back to C2 headquarters. It still felt strange being outside by herself. Granger had only just permitted that. He knew that she would always return. He would never let his three Operation IQ children out together. That way, he always had a hostage. Besides, she needed the secret chemical that her tiny nanites released to keep her brain working. She was tied to C2.

You're an important scientific experiment, Granger once told her.

Jesse snorted. *I'm NOT an experiment. I'm a girl.*

As her mind drifted, her eyes scanned the street around her for signs that she was being tailed. *None.*

It was an hour's walk to Walter's apartment. Jesse didn't mind. The air was heavy with cooking aromas. She sniffed, then tried to guess which meal was being prepared. Then she imagined the families that might be waiting to eat it.

A line of yawning commuters waited at a bus stop. Some read books, others chatted, a few stared blankly at nothing. A gust of wind fluttered dresses and ruffled hair. A woman sneezed. Jesse smelled dust. A tall man in a dark suit lost his grip on his newspaper. The wind whipped it from his fingers, scattering pages.

One page blew against Jesse's shins. Another caught on her chest. She snatched up half a dozen pages. The wind whisked the remainder from her reach.

"Here. Sorry they're a bit messed up." Jesse shrugged as she offered the rescued pages to the man. The wind flapped them as though it were teasing her.

"Thanks, but I've read it." He made no move to take it from her. "You have it."

And people think I'm *weird!*

The bus arrived and the man boarded along with the other commuters.

Jesse looked down at the pages in her hand. *What am I — a walking trash can?*

A small article caught her attention.

"RUBBER GIRL" IN ACCIDENT

An unidentified girl about 12 years of age tangled with a car this afternoon. And the girl won.

As Horatio Yeats drove his new Toyota Camry down Calendula Avenue, he was surprised by a girl who ran on to the road.

"She came out of nowhere," said Yeats. "I couldn't stop. She hit the hood and rolled forward. I drove right over her. It was terrible. I'll have nightmares about it for a long time, I can tell you." The unconscious girl was rushed to St. Mark's Hospital.

Doctors say she has temporary amnesia from the blow to her head. Amazingly, she has no other injuries.

"It's a miracle," said bystander Judith Wesley. "She should have broken bones, internal injuries, something to show that a car ran over her. All she has is a bump on the head and a few scrapes. It's like she was made of rubber."

Jesse turned over that page. On the back was an interview with a man who claimed that aliens had inserted a tracking device up his right nostril.

She scrunched the sheets of newspaper and tossed them into the nearest trash can. *Sounds like those reporters make things up when they're bored.*

Had C2 ever considered putting tracers in people's noses? *If they do, I don't want the job.*

The farther she walked, the less crowded the streets became.

When she was just blocks from Walter's

place, her feet slowed as she passed several restaurants — Thai, Chinese, and Italian. Her mouth watered. She'd eaten Indian food once, but she hadn't tried Thai or Chinese.

Jesse patted her shoulder bag. She had cash from her allowance. She had an empty stomach. Why not eat? A thrill ran through her at this small freedom.

She paused to read a menu that was taped to the window of the Thai restaurant.

Someone inside stood up, followed by his companion.

Jesse gasped. She turned her face aside and moved to the edge of the large window. *Don't run. You'll attract attention.*

Leaning to the left, she peeked into the restaurant.

Two men faced each other, shouting and waving their arms. The younger man put one hand on his companion's arm. The older man brushed him away and headed for the door.

Jesse ducked around the corner into a dark alley. *Why are Walter Preston and Director Granger together?*

20.

Jesse watched from the shadows.

Granger, with a face like a thunderstorm, climbed into a dark-blue car that was parked beside the curb. He accelerated into the traffic with a screech of tires.

Walter ignored him. He continued walking along the sidewalk toward his apartment.

Jesse waited till Walter crossed the street and was on the next block, then she followed him. It wasn't difficult. There were lots of streetlights. And Walter walked slowly, his white hair standing out like a pale beacon. Mingling with the pedestrians, she kept him in sight.

He stumbled, looked confused. Then he sat on a low brick wall.

Something's wrong with him.

Hurriedly, she caught up.

Did Granger do something to him? Slip something into his drink or meal? She'd heard of a man who died after a secret agent prodded him in the leg with an umbrella. The tip had been poisoned. If Walter and Granger were working together and the old man had become a threat, that would be one way to silence him.

Walter swayed on the brick wall like an aged Humpty Dumpty.

Alert, but appearing relaxed, she called out, "Hello, Walter."

Slowly he raised his head. Blinked. He didn't seem to recognize her at first, then she saw him nod. "Oh . . . Miriam."

"Miranda, actually." She smiled. "But if I wasn't called Miranda, I'd choose Miriam. It's different. I thought I saw you back there in the Thai restaurant. With a man in a suit."

Walter looked away. "I don't know anyone around here, except for Daniel. I keep to myself. I ate alone."

No, you didn't. "Walter, are you OK?"

He sighed. "I'm not the best. Something I ate, perhaps."

Uh-oh.

"I'm worn out. Can't sleep. They keep me awake most of the night."

"Who?"

A wary expression settled on his face. "You shouldn't worry your pretty little head about me. You only get one childhood. Enjoy it."

Jesse said nothing, but Walter would get a shock if he knew what her childhood was really like.

"The less you know, the better," he added.

She'd heard that before. It was a good excuse for keeping secrets. "I'll walk you home," she suggested, planning what to do if he fainted on the sidewalk.

He stood and took her arm in his.

Jesse froze, wondering if he was getting into position to throw her to the ground.

But Walter simply leaned on her a little. "Thank you, Miranda."

She smelled Asian spices on his breath. There was a brownish stain on the front of his shirt, where he'd splashed some of his dinner.

In silence, they walked to his apartment.

He managed the stairs better than she predicted. But they rested on each level.

Fumbling slightly, he began to unlock his door.

Jesse felt a rush of warm air as another door, behind them, swung open.

She spun around.

Daniel glared from across the corridor. His brown eyes blazed.

21.

"What are you doing to Walter?" demanded Daniel.

Jesse was half-tempted to say, *I'm hanging him off a bridge by his feet.* But she restrained herself. Just.

Walter made a *tsk tsk* sound with his tongue. "As a matter of fact, young man, Miranda has helped me home. I'm not feeling too chipper."

She looked hard at Daniel. *Is he trying to protect Walter — or pry me loose so he can get at him?* If Daniel was a genetically engineered Nimbus child, he was capable of anything.

Did Granger also know the boy Daniel? Jesse trusted Granger about as much as she'd trust an enraged death adder. If it was a choice between them, the adder would look pretty tempting.

"Have they . . . ?" Daniel bit off the rest of his words.

"Shh. Enough," said Walter, as he pushed open his door.

Jesse followed him inside. Daniel was right behind them.

There was a faint but lingering aroma of toast from earlier in the day. *He used butter.* Margarine had a different smell.

Daniel relocked Walter's front door and slid home the bolt and chain.

Uneasiness washed through Jesse. *Is he locking us in — or enemies out?*

"Sit down, Walter. I'll get you a hot drink," she said. "I know where everything is."

"What do you hear, Miranda?" asked Walter.

Daniel stood silent and glowering.

Jesse tilted her head to one side. "Traffic. Car horns. A television set. The wind whistling around the building."

"Is that all?"

She nodded, watching him curiously.

"Yes, of course." Walter nodded slowly.

What can you hear that I can't?

22.

Jesse entered the kitchen, filled the kettle, and put it on the stove.

Again, Daniel was right behind her.

"Would you like a drink, too, Daniel?"

He stepped closer, his stare intense and unblinking. "Who are you?"

"I told you. My name's . . ."

"That's not what I mean." He lowered his voice till it was more of a hiss. "Leave Walter alone. He's old. He can't hurt anybody."

Oh yes he can, thought Jesse, as the memory of the chocolate box with the fake anthrax surfaced.

Calmly, she took three mugs from the cupboard. "You're a rude boy, aren't you?"

He opened his mouth as if he was going to say something, then closed it again.

"My friend Jasmine told me that when a boy insults you, that means he likes you." She raised her eyebrows. "You know . . . in a *romantic* kind of way."

Daniel took a step backward.

"My mom says that girls sometimes like horses before they like boys, but we live in an apartment — so, you know, horses are not going to happen. But I do like dogs. We're allowed to have dogs in our apartment. My dog chews the heads off mice and he sheds hair, but I love him. So I guess I'm in the dog — not the boy — stage. Sorry."

Daniel looked totally confused. Which was just how Jesse wanted him to be. Sometimes the best defense was to attack. If you accused someone of something or became argumentative, they sometimes forgot their original complaint.

She leaned on the cupboard and eyeballed him. "You don't blink. Why is that?"

Daniel blinked, as though she'd just reminded him. His face flushed red.

Jesse decided that that was enough

needling to keep Daniel quiet for now. She called out, "Do you want an herbal infusion or a coffee, Walter?"

There was no answer.

She walked to the door and looked into the living room.

Abruptly, Walter leaped to his feet and grabbed the baseball bat from behind the door.

Suddenly, she realized the dangerous position she was in. Locked in a small apartment with a strange boy who hated her and a crazy old man wielding a bat.

23.

Walter began to beat the carpet as though he saw a rat or some other creature.

Jesse didn't know whether to speak up and distract him — or keep quiet in case he turned on her.

Daniel dashed to Walter. "What's the matter?"

He dropped the bat. It fell with a dull thump on the thick carpet. "There's nothing there, is there?"

"No," said Daniel and Jesse at the same time.

"What's happening to me?" Walter's face was distressed, confused. He grabbed the front of the boy's T-shirt. Daniel showed no fear. Jesse had to admire him for that. Walter looked crazy. The only thing missing was froth at his mouth.

"There's a plane. They're going to attack again."

Was he talking about the prints of old war planes on the wall, reliving his wartime experiences? She'd heard that old people did that sometimes. They couldn't remember things that happened yesterday, but they recalled exact details of events from years before.

"Don't go outside. Go home." He pushed Daniel. Not enough to hurt him, just enough to make him stagger back.

Walter pushed his hands over his ears. "No . . . I'm not listening."

It was like watching someone interact with the invisible man.

Suddenly Walter collapsed, as though the legs had been knocked from under him. His head hit the corner of the coffee table.

Jesse winced.

He bounced from the table to the carpet and lay still. A red stain pooled behind his head.

Daniel stood frozen.

"He's bleeding!" Jesse grabbed a dish towel from the kitchen and pressed it against Walter's scalp.

Daniel had not moved. His eyes seemed stuck in the wide-open position. He looked like the next one to pass out.

"Head wounds often bleed a lot. It might not be too serious," she told him quietly and calmly.

But the sight of Walter's blood on the carpet, on the towel, and matting his hair made her stomach flip-flop.

The hair on her arms stood up suddenly, as though a chill wind had tickled her skin. *Walter's chest isn't moving.* She held her fingers against his nostrils. *No air.* Then she pressed two fingers under his chin. *Zero pulse.*

24.

Jesse stood on the curb, searching for a familiar car. The glare of headlights was blinding.

She tapped her foot impatiently. *There it is, stopped at the red light. At last.* A wave of relief flooded through her. The lights changed and the battered vehicle turned toward her, slowing to a stop.

She opened the door and leaped inside. Her foot skidded on takeout containers that littered the floor. She wished Liam would stop taking the pickles out of his hamburgers and leaving them in the discarded wrappings. The smell had seeped into the upholstery. "Keep driving. I need to talk."

Liam looked over his shoulder, signaled, then accelerated out into the traffic. "You weren't followed?"

"Not that I could tell." She sighed. "And I looked really carefully."

"What's all the mystery?"

"I need help."

She half-expected a smart reply, but he simply nodded. *Maybe my face shows what I feel — panic!*

"Tell me everything."

She tilted her head to one side. *Everything? He's kidding.*

As if he'd read her thoughts he added, "OK. That was stupid. I forgot who we were for a moment. Secret agents never tell *everything*. Not even to each other."

His words gave Jesse a pang. He didn't know how right he was. Her mind was churning with everything that had happened in the last few days. She felt like a jug that was full of liquid and ready to spill over. Certainly the information that Rohan had given her was not to be shared with Liam. But maybe he already knew. And that was one of his own secrets.

"It's complicated." She didn't know where to start.

"Is this about the little whispers you and Granger had in his office?"

She half-turned to face Liam so she could see his reaction. "Granger gave me a job to do and I wasn't supposed to tell anyone. *Anyone.* He insisted. But it's all a mess. Walter Preston, the man I was supposed to be checking out, dropped dead and I had to revive him."

Liam's hands tightened momentarily on the steering wheel. "That's certainly a complication."

"It gets worse," she said. "This man's fingerprints were on that chocolate box we found in the station. He used to work for our government."

Liam looked at her then, his eyes showing surprise. "And Granger sent you in alone?"

"Tonight I saw the man, Walter, with Granger in a Thai restaurant. They didn't see me, though. Granger didn't say he knew Walter. Walter claimed he was in the restaurant alone. They had a big argument. Then, when I followed Walter home, I could see he was sick. He said that it might have been something he . . . ate."

"I see. Do you think Granger tried to take him out?"

"What if they were working together? If Walter planted the fake anthrax, then maybe Granger is involved. But why would he call himself to give the warning?"

"If there was actually a call. We only have Granger's word for that. It came through on his direct line."

A light shower of rain made the road glisten in the lights. Liam flicked on the windshield wipers.

"It's all so weird." She told him about the apartment upstairs, Daniel, and the fake homeless man.

"Tell me again about the way Walter behaved."

Jesse listed all the odd things Walter had said and done, and how he had looked.

"I have an idea. I've seen this kind of thing before."

"What, insanity?"

"Seen plenty of that." Liam braked to allow a woman to cut in. She hadn't looked.

"But this man may not be insane. Someone might want us to think that. But I'd need to check it out before I say anything more."

"Will you do that for me?"

"Sure. What are partners for?"

Once, Jesse had distrusted Liam. Disliked him. Certainly, at first, he had resented having a girl for a partner. He was worried that she'd get him killed. But Liam had helped bring Rohan back and said nothing. Asked for nothing in return. He was not the one who had betrayed her. She thought of what Rohan had told her about his discovery in the hacked C2 computer files, and she felt a pang.

"Do you mind going to the apartment on your own?" she asked. "I have to go to the hospital to check on Walter."

She remembered the perspiration soaking her back and the ache in her arms as she compressed Walter's chest and breathed life into his lungs with mouth-to-mouth resuscitation.

Then she'd screamed at Daniel to snap him into action. "Call an ambulance. *Now!*"

Daniel had dropped the phone, fumbled

the number. He shook like a leaf trembling in the wind. Either he was an unbelievably brilliant actor or he was genuinely upset.

Suddenly Jesse's wrist communicator, disguised as a watch, vibrated an alert.

Liam looked down at his own watch. "Uh-oh. Something's up."

She checked the text message. "Headquarters wants us back. *Now.*"

25.

Legs pumping, Jesse dashed through the C2 underground parking garage.

Liam had dropped her ten minutes from headquarters. Then they would arrive separately at the meeting. Granger would not suspect she had involved Liam against his orders.

Although the idea sounded good when Liam suggested it, Jesse was now regretting it. It took longer than she had anticipated to cover the distance.

Someone called her name as she sprinted across the parking garage, skirting cars. She heard the voice clearly, recognized it. But pretended she hadn't. She didn't look around or slow down. *Not now. I can't face it. And I don't have time.* Jesse had questions, but now wasn't the time to ask them. Not till the mystery of Walter and the anthrax scare was sorted out.

She pressed her palm against the identification pad. The elevator doors opened, then closed quickly behind her. She bent over, sucking air into her lungs.

Minutes later she slipped inside the briefing room. Fifty men and women were packed inside, watching a large plasma TV screen.

Granger sent an acid glare in her direction.

So I'm a few minutes late. Send a helicopter next time. She wiped perspiration from her brow and smoothed down her damp bangs.

Liam ignored her, as though her entrance was of no interest.

Easing to the back of the room, she stood quietly and listened.

The TV reporter was a young woman with large teeth. She clutched a microphone and aimed a concerned expression toward the camera. ". . . I have the Police Commissioner, Jonathon Martini, with me now."

A tall thin man in uniform, looking equally grave, stepped forward.

"So what's being done about this threat, Commissioner?"

"Sally, we've canceled all flights in and out of the city."

Jesse looked around the room. All eyes were fixed on the screen.

"This could be a hoax, but we're not taking any chances," said the Commissioner.

"But what about small planes from outlying airports?" Sally thrust the microphone at Commissioner Martini again. He moved his head back slightly, as though he feared she'd knock it against his teeth.

Heat shot through Jesse like a jolt of electricity. *Planes?*

"We have officers, uniformed and plain-clothes, on their way to all airports."

"But there are hundreds of private planes out there, owned by companies or farmers. What about those?"

Commissioner Martini smiled, but it was plastic. It was the fakest smile Jesse had ever seen. But what could the man do when he was cornered on national television? "I want people to know that we are making every effort to protect them. They should remain calm."

There was a ripple of restlessness around the room.

She was tempted to nudge the woman next to her and ask what was happening, but held herself back. *Don't draw attention to yourself, Jesse.*

The camera zoomed in on Sally, the toothy reporter, again. "To recap our scoop — about an hour ago, our station received a phone call from a person who says they intend spreading anthrax across the city via an airplane at midday tomorrow. At this time, no demands have been made. Now let's switch to our medical expert to learn about anthrax."

Granger pointed the remote at the screen and switched it off. The room was heavy with shocked silence.

Jesse thought of Walter. *There's a plane,* he'd said earlier in the evening. *They're going to attack again.*

26.

The door's locked. Jesse stood outside St. Mark's Hospital, gritting her teeth with annoyance. Visiting hours were over.

Getting to the hospital had been slow. The roads were packed with cars, bicycles, trucks, buses, and motorcycles as people fled the city. Long lines snaked along the sidewalks outside the train stations. Yet there were only a few pedestrians. Those who could not flee the city were battening down at home, windows shut, doors locked.

Panic itself had created chaos. Even before any contamination by anthrax. And if anthrax was dispersed over the city, many would become ill. Many would die.

How am I going to get in there to see Walter? If he's still alive. She hadn't resuscitated anyone before. But he had a heartbeat when they put him into the ambulance.

If Walter was involved in this latest anthrax threat, he had information that might allow C2 to stop it. But he couldn't fly a plane from his hospital bed. No matter how clever he was. He must be working with others. Maybe Nimbus. Maybe another group. A memory of Walter arguing with Granger in the restaurant surfaced.

What if Granger was setting up Walter, making him look guilty? If she could find out what Walter really knew, then she would decide what step to take next.

I want results, Granger had told her in the briefing room after he issued assignments to the other agents. C2 eyes and ears would be all over the city. *See me in my office at nine a.m. tomorrow. And I suggest you have a definite answer — is Walter Preston involved in these bioweapon threats or not?* His blue eyes had gone as cold and hard as his voice. When he *suggested* in that tone, it was an order. In fact, it was more than that. He'd sounded almost desperate.

Granger had given no sign that he suspected Walter was ill. She'd kept the latest development to herself till she knew if Granger was involved.

A taxi pulled to a stop beside her at the hospital. A man with a bandage tied around one leg climbed out. He paid the driver, shook his head, then limped painfully toward the doors. The man was overweight, and struggled painfully to take the few necessary steps to reach the buzzer.

Swiftly, Jesse moved to his side. "Let me help you. Lean on me. I'm pretty strong. I do karate."

The man's strained features relaxed. "Is that so? Thank you, young lady. I won't need your karate tonight. Just your shoulders." He leaned one arm across her shoulders and used her as a kind of crutch.

"I'm here to visit my uncle." She pressed the buzzer.

"Maybe a hospital is the safest place to be at the moment."

Jesse knew he was referring to the anthrax threat, but she said nothing.

A male nurse opened the door. "If you're here for an anthrax vaccination, we're out of serum. Sorry."

Already had mine, thought Jesse. Then she felt a stab of guilt for all the people who were not vaccinated.

The man pointed to his bandaged knee. "I cut myself with an electric saw." The tight line of his lips showed that he was in pain. And the widening red stain on his makeshift bandage indicated that the wound needed immediate attention.

"I'll get a wheelchair," said the nurse.

Jesse helped the injured man into a chair. He rested his head in his hands.

Silently she eased away, putting distance between them, then slipped around a corner into an empty hallway.

27.

The door to Walter's room opened. Someone was coming out.

Jesse ducked from the hallway into the room opposite. The body-shaped lump under the covers snored gently.

Jesse smelled light, floral perfume. *Must be a female. She's as thin as a pancake. That figures. Healthy people don't stay in hospitals.*

Opening the door just a crack, Jesse peeked out. Daniel was leaving Walter's room. A man with a stethoscope around his neck passed him from the opposite direction. "Daniel Rubinstein!"

The boy looked up.

"Are you sick again?" asked the doctor. "What are you doing here?"

Ah, so Daniel's been here before.

He shrugged. "I'm just visiting a friend, Dr. Fuller."

"How is your friend?"

Smiling, Daniel said, "He's going to be all right." There was such a genuine look of relief on his face that Jesse believed he meant it.

The doctor took Daniel's chin in his hands. "You haven't been putting enough drops in those eyes."

"I forget sometimes."

"How's everything else?"

Daniel nodded.

"Glad to hear that. You need to take care. Had a man in here last week who'd chopped his finger clean off and didn't realize it till his wife complained about blood on the tiles. Like you, he had Riley-Day syndrome."

Daniel took a small step to show he wanted to leave. "I have to go now, Dr. Fuller. My aunt's picking me up."

Riley-Day. That explained Daniel's symptoms. Riley-Day patients were born with a mutation of chromosome 9. Daniel's sweating, his short stature, the blotching, insensitivity to pain, even his dry eyes were symptoms. Suddenly Jesse felt sad. Half of the Riley-Day patients didn't live past twenty. Any that reached forty were considered old. Daniel had no hope of reaching Walter's age.

If Daniel was undergoing regular medical tests in a public hospital, then he was not a genetically altered Nimbus child. The doctors here would find out. Nimbus would not permit that. Daniel was not a mutant. He was simply a sick boy who was trying to protect his friend, Walter Preston.

Suddenly Jesse focused on the room she was in, listening carefully. There was a faint squelching sound.

Slowly, she let the door close. There was still light filtering in through the curtains.

Expecting trouble, Jesse half-turned.

The lights shining through the curtains were not the only source of illumination in the room. A girl was propped up on one elbow.

She seemed to be glowing herself. Her arms, face, and neck were fluorescent.

She was larger than her sleeping form had suggested. Her voice cracked when she spoke, "Have you come to kill me?"

28.

Jesse was stunned.

Then she heard footsteps outside the door — not the confident stride of a hospital worker, but the light, careful footsteps of someone who was sneaking around.

Hot pins and needles shot across the back of her neck.

Jesse put one finger to her lips to signal the other girl to be quiet. She scanned the room, looking for a place to hide. She tugged at the closet door, but it was locked.

Slowly, the door of the room began to open.

The girl in the bed plopped back and pulled the covers up to her chin.

Jesse threw herself under the bed, sliding through a film of dust. She could smell it, taste it in her mouth. *I thought these places were cleaned every day.* She pressed one finger to her top lip, just beneath her nose, to stop a sneeze.

The nanites in her brain accentuated and improved certain skills. Her eyesight, for one. Jesse could see better in the dark than the average person. *That's a woman standing there.*

Dressed in dark clothing, the woman tilted her head, listening.

Although it seemed a long wait to Jesse, she knew it was only seconds.

Something flashed in the woman's hand. A syringe?

Jesse held her breath, afraid that any sound or movement would give away her hiding place.

Nurses didn't sneak into rooms in the dark to administer needles. They switched on lights. They chattered. They clomped about like elephants.

Jesse thought of the girl in the bed above her. *I might not have come in here to kill you, but someone else has.*

Wait. Don't move too quickly, she told herself.

Suddenly, the woman pounced.

But Jesse was primed. Her hands snaked out from under the bed, grabbed the woman's ankles, and tugged.

The woman tumbled backward.

Jesse scrambled out from beneath the bed. In one swift, smooth movement, she pulled a can from her shoulder bag and sprayed the woman in the face.

Immediately, the woman went limp. She would be unconscious for a while, but would suffer no permanent damage.

Jesse spun around to check on the girl in the hospital bed. "Are you OK?"

"Yes, but we'd better get out of this room. They work in pairs. If she doesn't report back that she's been successful, her partner must complete the job."

Complete the job? That's a tidy way of talking about murder.

29.

The girl pushed back the covers and got out of bed.

She and Jesse were about the same height. When they faced each other, they were eye to eye.

"My name's Tamarind," whispered the girl, as she flicked on a bedside light. She had smooth, pale skin and blonde hair. Her eyes were sea-blue.

She took a key from her bedside drawer, stepped over the unconscious woman sprawled on the floor, and opened the closet door. "My clothes are in here." She looked down at the bright pink teddy bear pajamas.

"I'd be a bit obvious in these. What's your name?"

Jesse opened her mouth to give a made-up name, as she usually did. But something stopped her. "Jesse."

"Is that your real name?" asked Tamarind. She hurriedly dragged a pair of blue jeans and a red sweater over her pajamas.

Jesse nodded. "And you?"

"Yes. Tamarind is my birth name."

"You were glowing. Now you've stopped. You're from Nimbus." Jesse was so certain, she didn't even frame it as a question.

Tamarind paused, with one sock on and one sock off.

"I've met one of your girls before," Jesse explained.

Nodding, Tamarind pulled on the second sock and took out her sneakers. "C2?"

"Yes." What was the point in lying?

Jesse stomped on the syringe, smashing it to pulp. Then she eased open the door to check the hallway. For now, it was clear.

"Who's that woman?" she asked Tamarind.

"A Nimbus assassin."

"Why does she want to kill you?"

"Because I'm a security risk. I was hit by a car and knocked unconscious. An ambulance brought me here before I woke up. I couldn't do anything about it. The doctors did blood tests and soon they'll get the results and then they'll know . . . things about me."

So this is the "rubber girl" from that news-paper article.

"When they brought me in I was unconscious. I hit my head. Then I got a bit upset and insisted they let me go. But they wouldn't because a responsible adult hadn't come to identify me. They gave me something to make me sleep. I only just woke up." She yawned.

"You're genetically engineered," said Jesse.

Tamarind didn't bluster or cover up. She looked relieved, as though she was tired of hiding who she really was.

Jesse understood how she felt.

"My mother was a human cell and my father was a glow-in-the-dark blob that floated in the ocean. They met in a test tube."

"Your father was *what*?"

"I have human and jellyfish genes. That's why I glow when I'm scared."

"Oh."

"If I'm dead, I can't talk. Nimbus won't take any chances. Secrecy is everything."

Jesse could also identify with that remark. The Nimbus and C2 organizations were similar in some ways.

She could not imagine what anyone at C2 would say about her rescuing a member of Nimbus. Despite the fact that she hadn't known the other girl's origins when she helped her.

Tamarind's fingers moved rapidly over her sneaker laces. "Let's get out of here."

"I can't leave the hospital yet. I have something important to do." Jesse thought of Walter, in the opposite room. The anthrax threat had not gone away.

She looked again at the woman out cold on the floor. Professional killers were after Tamarind. But tomorrow, at midday, professional killers would try to take out a whole city. And in a slow, horrible way.

30.

Jesse creaked open the door. From the darkness of Tamarind's room, she looked left, then right along the hallway.

At the beginning of the hallway, a nurse pushed a metal cart.

Tamarind leaned forward. "She'll be gone in a second. I'll bolt then."

"No! Look at her shoes."

There was a tense silence. "She's not a nurse, is she?"

"Definitely not." The uniform was correct. But the grubby sneakers were not.

"What do we do?" asked Tamarind.

"Keep calm. Think about something nice,"

said Jesse. "If you get upset, you'll glow, and that'll help give you away."

"Right." Tamarind took a breath. "Except I don't have any nice thoughts. The only one I have is about getting away. And I can't do that with a Nimbus assassin in the hallway."

Jesse looked at her. Tamarind had a haze of light about her body. "Think about us both being weird. You're part jellyfish and I'm an artificially produced prodigy."

"That's a nice thought?"

"Yes. It means we can be friends. We don't have to bother explaining to each other, or hiding that we're weird. We know we are."

As Jesse watched, the glow on Tamarind's skin faded. *So she likes that idea.*

"What are we going to do?" Tamarind whispered. "She'll be armed."

"I can do tae kwon do and karate. I've got knockout spray. And I've got you." Jesse wished she felt as confident as she sounded. But it wouldn't help if the other girl panicked.

"Nurse." A voice came from the other end of the hallway.

Surprised, the Nimbus imposter stopped.

She couldn't ignore the call. It would look suspicious.

"Yes?"

An orderly began to search through the items on the cart.

The Nimbus woman turned to talk to him.

"Now!" Jesse grabbed Tamarind's hand and dashed across the hallway into Walter's room.

By the night-light, they could see that someone was asleep in the bed.

"Now what?" whispered Tamarind.

"We can't run the whole length of the hallway with her there. But if she sees the room is empty, she might think you've already escaped. When the coast is clear, you can leave."

"But we can't stay. There's someone in here."

"Yes, I know." Jesse beckoned Tamarind closer to Walter.

Together, they stood beside his sleeping body. Although there was a bandage around his head, his breathing was steady and strong.

"Do you know who this is?" asked Jesse.

Tamarind was from Nimbus. Would she recognize Walter?

But she looked genuinely puzzled. "No. I've never seen him before. Has he hurt his head?" Her gaze was straight. Her voice firm.

Jesse believed Tamarind was telling the truth. "His name's Walter. And I can't leave till I've interrogated him."

31.

Jesse's wrist communicator vibrated an alert. *Busy day.*

Tamarind carried a chair across to the door and sat on it, blocking entrance to the room.

The illuminated display on the communicator showed Jesse a text message from Liam. He'd uncovered some vital facts.

Jesse looked at Walter. His eyes were firmly closed. This might be the first undisturbed sleep he'd had in some time. *Sorry.* She switched on the bed light and shook his arm. "Wake up, Walter. It's . . ." she threw an apologetic glance across at Tamarind. "It's Miranda."

Walter blinked, once, twice, then his eyelids popped wide open.

"Oh, hello. You've brought a friend. How nice. Daniel was here earlier. He told me what you did. I . . . thank you, my dear." He took her hand and squeezed it. "You saved my life."

"She's good at that," said Tamarind.

"Walter, I have to ask you some questions. It's really important."

He let go of Jesse's hand and fixed his pale blue eyes on her. "Fire away."

"Before you collapsed in the apartment, you said something about planes attacking. What did you mean?"

He half-closed his eyes, hesitated. "I don't remember. Why are you asking me about that? You're an agent, aren't you?"

"Yes, Walter. You probably haven't heard about it, but someone contacted the media and threatened to spread anthrax across the city, tomorrow, from a plane."

Jesse was aware that Tamarind sat absolutely still, like a statue. If she was from Nimbus, she might know about the threat.

But maybe not. There were many people doing all kinds of secret work for C2. Jesse wouldn't recognize them if they stood on her toes, and she had no idea what they were involved in.

Walter rubbed his face with one hand. "If I talk about what's in my head, they'll lock me up and throw away the key. I'll never get out. I couldn't stand it. I must be able to see the sky and look after my plants."

Jesse leaned closer, forcing him to meet her gaze. "Lots of people might die if you don't help us."

"I want to help, but I don't know anything."

"Well, I can tell *you* something, Walter. My friend has been searching the apartment above yours."

"Mrs. Sugars' apartment? She went to Paris for six months. There's no one up there."

"Someone's been up there, Walter," said Jesse. "They recorded your phone messages, bugged your apartment. You were right about that homeless man. He was a fake.

You are *not* going mad. Someone wanted you to think that. They wanted others to think that."

"But I see things." Walter's face creased with anxiety. "I hear them."

"Yes, you do. My friend discovered that the apartment above yours used a huge amount of electricity in the past month. He found what looked like a microwave oven." Jesse remembered seeing it in the kitchen, but she'd paid no attention to it. But Liam had seen these devices before. He knew what to look for. It wasn't simply an oven.

"Someone's been directing microwaves into your apartment through the ceiling. They put pictures in your mind. And words. You couldn't tell what were your own thoughts and what was planted there. Your mind was invaded."

Walter moved restlessly against his pillow.

"It was you who phoned about the anthrax simulant, wasn't it?"

His eyes flared with panic. "I didn't put it there. I just knew about it. The words came into my head. I had to tell someone. But I was afraid they'd either assume I was involved or that I'm losing my mind. I'm old, so it's easy to believe that I'm senile." He snorted. "What am I saying? *I* thought I was losing my mind, too."

"Your fingerprints were found on the box containing the powder. Someone wants you to take the blame."

If someone had tried to make Walter look crazy or guilty, they'd give him just enough information to incriminate himself, but not enough for him to stop the attack. It was a clever plan. Walter had been a biologist. He knew about bioweapons. He was the perfect choice.

But there was one question left to ask. "I saw you talking to that man in the restaurant. Tell me about him."

He sighed, then shrugged. "He sent you, didn't he?"

"What connection is there between you?"

"I told him to stay away, that all this would mess things up for him. If he told his people that I was the informant, they'd blame him. But if he didn't tell and they found out, he'd still carry the blame. Now there's a second threat, he'll look suspicious for covering up the first." His fingers plucked at the cotton blanket that covered him.

"So he's not trying to hurt you?"

Walter laughed gently. "No. In his own twisted way he's trying to protect me. Theodore Granger is my son."

32.

"Call security!" came the shout from the hospital hallway outside Walter's room.

Jesse was instantly alert. *Either they've found the Nimbus assassin out cold on the floor or the second one's causing trouble.*

Tamarind's eyes widened with terror.

Walter switched off the light without waiting to be asked. The remaining glow from the night-light created an eerie atmosphere.

Jesse saw him glance at Tamarind, then turn his head for a second look.

She patted his arm. "Don't ask, Walter." She knew he was wondering about Tamarind's peculiar glow.

He nodded. "I learned years ago, when

my son got into that secret business, to ignore all kinds of wacky things. Not that you're wacky, dear. Merely interesting."

You don't know the half of it, Walter. "We have to go," said Jesse. "Act dumb."

"That should be no problem." He snuggled down against his pillow, imitating sleep. "I still owe you a chocolate mint cutting. Stop by and collect it some time."

Jesse raced to the window. *Yes, there's a ledge.* She slid up the screen. The window swung outward on a hinge. There was enough room to climb through, but the narrow ledge was a worry.

Urgently, Jesse whispered, "Tamarind, move the chair from the door. It'll look suspicious." Then she beckoned the other girl over to the window.

"We're three floors up," whispered Tamarind.

"I know. But it's the window or the hallway. Take your pick." Within seconds Jesse was standing on the ledge, with a breeze tickling her neck. She shivered. The air was noisy with traffic sounds. Car horns blared. Then a siren wailed.

Jesse helped Tamarind onto the ledge. She pushed down the screen and leaned on the window to close it.

They had to move. If anyone looked out, they would see them clinging to the wall.

Although it was night, there were plenty of lights. "Let's go left," suggested Jesse. "We're near the corner and there's a fire escape. We can use the outside stairs."

Palms flat against the rough wall, Jesse shuffled along the ledge.

"Don't look down," she told Tamarind, and then had to stop herself doing the same thing. It made her feel woozy.

The wind whipped around them. But they continued inching toward the fire escape stairs.

"You're doing so much to help and you don't even know me," said Tamarind. "I could be here to trap you."

A jolt shot through Jesse. She didn't want to believe that. Yet it was possible. "Are you?"

"No. But I could be. We both know how things work in our organizations."

"Watch out for that dark patch," said Jesse. "It's bird droppings and it's slippery."

Tamarind obeyed. She was progressing, but she was breathing faster. Her skin glowed.

"Someone just tried to kill you. That's a big hint that they don't want you back," said Jesse. "For now, I'm stuck in C2. But I still have to be myself, as much as I can. I want to be the best person I can, even though I can't change some things about my life. My C2 partner says that life is like a game of cards. You're dealt a hand, and you can't change the cards. But it's up to you how you play the game."

"He sounds smart."

"He's not. He got that out of a book. His hair looks like yellow lawn. His car's a stinky mess. And he eats hamburgers all the time."

"Are you allowed to eat hamburgers?"

"No. But we're trained to keep secrets." Jesse clung to the drainpipe and peered around the corner. Disappointment struck her like a slap in the face.

"What's wrong?" asked Tamarind.

"There's a security guard on the stairs. We can't go that way."

Out of the blue, she sensed fluttering

wings. Something stuck in her hair, struggling and flapping. *Gross. A bat. No, it's a moth.* Instinctively, she shook her head, desperate to shake the thing loose. Her right foot slipped. She flailed her arms, knowing it was useless. *I'm falling!*

33.

A cool hand whipped out and wrapped around Jesse's wrist. She felt herself hauled in like a fish on a line.

She heard a faint squelching sound.

Suddenly, unexpectedly, she found herself firmly back on the ledge, hugging the wall. Sweat trickled down her spine, making her skin prickle. *Three floors is a long way to fall.*

She turned her head to look at the other girl. "What . . . what just happened?"

There was another squelch. Tamarind's left arm shrank back into her sleeve. She shrugged her shoulders as though she were relaxing muscles. "I'm not just a pale face, you know. Nimbus engineered me to have certain abilities."

"Don't tell me. You're also a good swimmer."

"Amazing."

"Can you communicate with fish?"

"Nah. They mostly want to eat me." Tamarind flashed a smile.

Jesse shook her head. This was so bizarre, unbelievable. Yet she had just seen Tamarind's flexibility at work.

"Let's cruise. I'm sick of this place. It's drafty." Jesse grabbed the drainpipe and shinnied to the level below, and the next, till her feet touched the ground.

Tamarind followed. Her glow had faded, leaving her skin looking pale but not abnormal.

Together they ran across the parking garage and the manicured lawn, then hopped a fence.

When they were safely away from the hospital, surrounded by trees in a park, they stopped running and caught their breath. The air was heavy with the scent of pine trees and some kind of sweet flower. Jesse suspected that there was also a full Dumpster close by. The park was empty.

"Where are you going now?" Jesse asked Tamarind. "They'll still be looking for you."

Tamarind shrugged. "I'll be fine."

Jesse recognized an expression that Liam often wore. "You have that *I don't have a plan* look."

"Could be because I don't have a plan."

"I thought so."

Tamarind leaned back against a tree and sighed. "I can look after myself. Tonight I was slow, groggy from the drugs they gave me. But my head's clear now."

"What will you do?"

"I don't know. It won't take people long to realize that I'm odd. As soon as I'm scared, I'll glow. And that's not the only difference."

Jesse sniffed. "Yeah, I saw the hand stretch thing."

"I won't fit in. What are they going to do with me? Take me to concerts and wave me over their heads like a glow stick?"

Jesse stifled a giggle. Tamarind might be funny, but she had a serious problem.

"What if I came back to C2 with you?" asked Tamarind.

"Whoa. Do you know what you're saying?"

Tamarind put one hand on Jesse's arm. "It can't be worse than Nimbus."

"They'll bug your room."

"So what's new?"

"They'll stick vitamin needles in you. Make you work out. They'll want to know about you. They'll do tests in the laboratory."

Tamarind nodded. "Used to that."

"Mary Holt, our carer, will make you eat organic vegetables, bran, and lentils."

"Oh, not *lentils*." She squeezed her chin between two fingers. "That might change things . . . but seriously, Jesse. I'll be alive. And I'll be with other weirdos."

Don't hold back, girlfriend.

"But this Granger person might not take me in. He'd have his own assassins. I could be in just as much danger."

Jesse smirked. "Well, he owes me big time. I saved his father's life, found out he was being harassed, not plotting bioterrorism. Besides, you'd have information you can give Granger. Like an exchange. He's eager to find out more about Nimbus. You don't have to say anything about your friends. Keep that to yourself."

"I don't have that many friends. Some of the other children have been engineered to have no feelings. It's like hanging out with zombies."

"I met one of them. Scary."

"And Nimbus keeps us on the move, in small groups." Tamarind's face sobered. She wrapped her arms around her body. "Will the anthrax attack really happen?"

"If we can't stop it. But the airports are closed. The air force is on the alert for any planes flying near the city. Even a toy soldier wouldn't get past them."

"Toys. That's it!" Tamarind smacked her forehead with one hand. "I know how they're going to do it."

34.

Music speakers bellowed into the all-night hamburger joint. Director Granger winced at the sound.

Too bad. Jesse had selected this table so the music would cover their conversation if anyone was trying to electronically eavesdrop.

Granger gave his hamburger a look that suggested it was made from fungus.

Jesse scanned the café. There were only a few customers. Outside, the stream of cars continued. The lines still moved slowly. Every few minutes, someone would lose patience and toot the horn, gesture, or shout out of the car windows. But it made no difference.

The traffic didn't move any faster. Most of those people would not make it out of town in time.

"I believe I owe you thanks, Jesse," said Granger. "Walter . . . my father . . . called me from the hospital and told me what happened. He would have died without your help."

"I'm glad Walter's all right." Jesse sipped her drink. "Why do you have different last names?"

"My parents divorced when I was a child. My mother married again and I took my stepfather's name."

Jesse could not picture Granger as a happy little boy playing with toy cars or building blocks.

"I thought it was better to meet here. Away from C2. The hospital's not safe, and neither is Walter's apartment." Jesse leaned forward. "I have important information about the anthrax threat."

Granger fixed both eyes on her. "Shoot."

She blinked.

"Perhaps I should rephrase that," he said. "Tell me what you know." He looked at his watch. "There are not many hours left till midday."

"I met a girl from Nimbus. She doesn't like what they're doing and she wants to help. I believe she's telling the truth. She was running away from Nimbus when she was hit by a car. . . . It's a long story. Nimbus has sent out assassins to kill her. But I found her first."

"Lucky for her," said Granger. "And perhaps for us." His eyes narrowed. "Where is this girl?"

"Close. She's waiting for my signal."

Granger tilted his head to one side. "Jesse Sharpe. Are you saying you don't trust me?"

"I'm being careful. This girl's scared and not sure about talking to you. And she's genetically engineered to have special abilities."

A gleam appeared in Granger's eyes.

"She wants a promise of protection from C2. She might not survive on her own if Nimbus is after her."

He peered through the dirty windows into the night. "Bring her in."

"Not yet. You haven't promised. Also, she's . . . um . . ."

Granger raised one eyebrow.

"She kind of glows when she's scared."

He tapped his fingertips together. "What does she know about the anthrax?"

"She hasn't given me details. She's waiting for your decision."

35.

Hidden by bushes, Jesse lay flat on her stomach. Holding binoculars with gloved hands, she scanned the slope leading to the reservoir. She hoped her camouflage gear would make her indistinguishable from the undergrowth.

Tamarind lay beside her, also peering through binoculars.

Keep by her side at all times, in case this is a setup. Trust must be earned, Granger had told her. *You brought her in. She's your responsibility.*

Jesse didn't mind. She had a new friend. One who intended to stay.

Lowering her binoculars, Tamarind whispered into Jesse's ear. "What if my guess is wrong and they don't show up?" Her breath fanned Jesse's hair.

Jesse whispered back, "Run. Fast. And I'll be right behind you."

Tamarind gave a tight smile, then checked her watch.

Exposed skin was a risk with infectious material, but their overalls were thick — and hot. Jesse felt perspiration dribble down her back.

Today's operation involved groundwork. C2 could not risk sending in planes or helicopters. Besides the danger of a trigger-happy air force pilot shooting them down, it would signal to Nimbus that its real plan had been discovered.

"No one would have guessed this was the target site, Tamarind. This reservoir holds the water supply for most of the city. You've saved a lot of lives."

While all eyes turned toward the sky, Nimbus coolly planned to infect the city's water supply. It was clever. Like a magician's sleight of hand. *What do you see in my right hand?* All the while, the object was actually hidden in the left. Watchers were distracted by a gesture or sound in another direction.

People left in the city were running around like crazed ants before rain. Nimbus made sure that those who were not infected by anthrax would be hysterical with fear. *What a mess!*

A sweet blackbird call echoed across the trees.

Silently, Jesse gestured to Tamarind. That bird call was a C2 signal that they had company.

Every second they waited was an agony. *What if Tamarind's wrong? What if we mess up and Nimbus carries out their plan?*

When Tamarind told Granger about the purchase of model airplanes, the hours of practice in the national park near the reservoir, it made a weird kind of logic. They were using planes all right, but not real ones. Rather, a fleet of model airplanes — ones that were strong enough to fly down over the reservoir.

They've been in the shop for special modifications, Tamarind had reported. Jesse had no doubt what those modifications would be.

Some device for spreading a slurry of infectious material.

She nudged Tamarind.

They pulled on their gas masks. Now they were totally covered. In that instant, they lost their human look. No faces, no expression. On her last assignment Jesse had seen Liam wearing a mask like this. He'd looked like a mutant pig. *Glad I don't have a mirror,* thought Jesse.

She grabbed Tamarind's wrist. She heard something in the thick trees behind them. A van. It cruised closer. The driver was not racing or sloughing over the rough track. He was careful, quiet, not drawing attention.

The van stopped. Its door slid open, Jesse turned her head in that direction, listening carefully. *Feet. Soft voices.* Nimbus was here.

36.

Jesse heard shouts. Then shots.

Tamarind went rigid. Jesse could feel waves of fear coming from her. Beneath that heavy outfit, she'd be shining.

There was a loud thump. The mayhem went on for several minutes. Jesse imagined the scene in her mind. The C2 agents had to be careful. Their mission was not just to capture the Nimbus group, but also to keep the anthrax material contained.

We need the Tamarind girl there, on site Granger had said, *but keep her away from the hot spot. We don't want her warning her colleagues.*

Despite the noisy action behind them,

Jesse looked through her binoculars again. "There's someone moving down there." She adjusted the binoculars. "Between those trees. Closer to the reservoir."

Tamarind looked through her binoculars. "That's Lyle." Her voice was muffled by the gas mask. "He's from Nimbus. What's he's got with him?"

Jesse hauled the binocular strap over her neck, let the glasses drop in the thick undergrowth. She scrambled to her feet. "It's a mobile rocket launcher."

Bent double, she dashed down through the bushes, darting left and right. Nimbus was trying a double sleight of hand. *Watch the skies, watch the model planes — no — watch the rocket. These guys don't give up!*

Small branches tried to grab her like arthritic hands. Twigs scraped her overalls. Suddenly she was grateful for their thickness. The mask concealed her side view. She could hear her own heavy breathing. It sounded bizarre, mechanical.

Jesse pushed her body as fast as it would go. There was no time to stop and message

Liam. If she called out, this Lyle from Nimbus would fire before she could get close enough.

She reached into her holster and took out a weapon. She'd had many hours' target practice. But she had never fired at a human.

The vegetation would soon give way to a smooth, lawn-covered slope. Accuracy would be hard if she shot while running, and he would see her coming. *I'll have to aim from the tree line.*

Abruptly, she reached the cleared section. Stopped.

Lyle stood by the water. He lifted the mobile rocket launcher up onto his shoulder.

Jesse aimed her weapon, took a deep breath, held it, then pressed the trigger.

37.

Jesse stood outside Director Granger's office, delaying her entrance. Her heart pounded at the thought of the confrontation to come.

The scanner inspected her retinas.

"Jesse Sharpe, you are cleared for entry," said the computer-generated voice. The doors to Granger's waiting room slid open. Jesse entered.

Prov wore a dark purple shirt today. Her thick brown hair was caught up in a loose knot on top of her head. Escaped curls dangled over her face. They gave her a soft, mother-of-the-year appearance. "Hello, honey. You're early. You'll have to wait a few minutes."

Jesse swallowed a lump in her throat and sat opposite Prov's desk.

An unusual silence stretched between them.

"Is everything OK?" Prov's soft brown eyes were wide with concern.

"How do you do that?" asked Jesse.

"Do what?"

"That look that makes it seem as though you care."

Prov blinked. The rest of her body was perfectly still.

"All this time I thought you cared about me," said Jesse.

"I . . . I do care. . . ."

"No, you don't. You can't." Jesse forced out the words. Part of her still wanted to disbelieve the secret that Rohan had discovered.

"I have a sister," said Jesse. She knew that revealing what she knew was a risk. If Prov told Granger, he would demand to know how Jesse had discovered the truth. But she was sick of secrets. She wanted some answers. *Needed* them.

"What a surprise."

"No, it isn't." Jesse eyeballed her. "You know how old she is, what she looks like. Because she looks just like me. She's my twin. Rohan, Jai, and me — we all have twins. That made the experiments really interesting, didn't it? Take one child, turn it into a genius. But let the other one grow up normally."

Prov shook her head.

"Even that time you gave me a copy of a newspaper report about the death of my parents — you were still lying. That wasn't the full article."

It was true that her parents had been killed in a car accident. It was also true that a baby girl was found alive at the site. But the missing part held the secret of another girl. Lost. She had disappeared from the accident scene without a trace. *That second girl was me.*

"Please don't lie to me now." Jesse sat forward. "Why did you do it?"

Prov sighed, long and hard. "It was years ago. I was a field agent then. I only did as I was told. I didn't give the order."

"But you carried it out. You could have

said no." Jesse knew that in every instance there was some kind of choice. Even if it was a small one. But not only had Prov stolen her from her family when she was only one year old, she had kept up the pretense all these years. Never given a clue.

"I was young. Ambitious. I didn't realize. Anyway, the three of you were truly orphans. There were no parents to miss you. Take Jai as an example. He was in an orphanage, a little refugee. At least here at C2 he'd have a better life than in that crowded camp."

Jesse snorted. Prov had obviously not spent much time in the laboratory.

"It began to eat away at me." Prov put one hand over her heart. "I stopped field assignments. I couldn't do that sort of thing anymore. There was an opening here, in the Director's office. I had children of my own. Then I realized what it meant to . . ."

"To steal someone from her family." Jesse thought of the years she had dreamed of relatives, imagined them, given them names. Her chest tightened painfully. It seemed so much worse that Prov had pretended to care.

"It was nothing personal," said Prov.

"Oh, it was personal. *Very* personal."

"Can you forgive me?" There was a tremor in Prov's voice. She seemed to have aged ten years in the last ten minutes.

Jesse was silent. She, too, had been involved in assignments that made her uncomfortable or frightened. She had wondered what would happen if C2 asked her to do something that was wrong. Maybe she had no right to be so angry. Yet years of a normal life had been taken from her.

Things were not always the way they appeared. Liam was not pretty to look at. He was impatient, had a sharp tongue. Yet he had stood by her, taken risks for her. And Prov? She had the pretty face and soft voice. Yet she had lied to Jesse all her life.

"I don't know if I can forgive you," said Jesse. "Maybe one day." She looked at Prov. *One day* might take a while to arrive.

38.

Granger gestured that Jesse should take a seat by his desk.

After her frank talk with Prov, Jesse felt mangled. She was in no mood for Granger's demands.

She sniffed gently. There was an unusual aroma in the office. Like mint.

Granger smoothed his tie. "So . . . your mission was successful. Anthrax threat averted. Walter Preston cleared. Nimbus cell captured. We're learning about their methods, how they think."

Jesse didn't want to know how they were extracting the information. She had a feeling that she wouldn't sleep if Granger gave details.

"The jellyfish girl knows more than she realizes."

"Tamarind," said Jesse. "Her name is Tamarind."

"She's settling in. Soon she'll be moved up to the residential floor with you and the boys." Granger pursed his lips. "You did well down at the reservoir. Perfect hit. There was enough tranquilizer in that dart to drop an elephant. And that fellow was built like one."

He reached down and picked up something from behind his desk. It was a small black pot with a plant in it. "Walter . . . my father . . . asked me to give you this."

A smile crept across Jesse's face. In her wildest dreams, she would never have imagined Director Granger offering her a chocolate mint plant.

The way he had tried to protect his father had been complicated. Silly, really. If he'd told her the truth, it would have been simpler, quicker. But Granger dealt in secrets. That's how he thought. But the incident with his father had revealed that he, too, was vulnerable, human. *Well, maybe just a little bit human.*

"My father's gone away for a while," said Granger. "Somewhere safe. To rest."

"That's a good idea."

"My father and I do not agree with each other on many matters. But he tried to protect me." He looked surprised, as though not many people would do something like that for him. "He was a perfect choice for the setup. He had the skills to be guilty. He was my father, and so if he was suspected of being a psychopathic killer, it would reflect on me. End my career." He cleared his throat. "Or worse."

"He cares about you," said Jesse.

"He'd arranged with that boy, Daniel, that he was to clear the apartment of any trace of our relationship in the event that something happened to him. And it almost did."

Jesse nodded. *So that's what they were talking about on the surveillance tape.*

"My father has been sharing his suspicions for years about outbreaks of viruses and diseases. He thinks that they're not all accidental." He rubbed one hand over his face, just the way Walter did. "But I wouldn't listen."

Granger stood up. "I think you should have a day off before your next assignment."

"Uh . . . OK." Jesse was suspicious. There was a strange look on his face.

"A day outside, in the sunshine. Get out of here for a while." Granger raised one eyebrow. "I know you'll come back."

Do I have a choice? I'd die without the C2 medication. My brothers are here. And now there's Tamarind.

"You're valuable to us, my dear."

Yeah, right. Heard this one. Usually just before you send me out to risk my life on some weird mission. Yet this time, Granger's voice did not carry its usual chill. He stood, tapped a file on his desk with his long white fingers. "I must speak to Providenza. I'll be gone. . . ." He looked at his watch. "Precisely ten minutes. I'd like you to wait here." He tapped the file a second time. Her eyes followed the sound.

Even upside down, she could read the file's title. "Jesse Sharpe. Top Secret. Eyes only."

Her eyes shot up to meet his. He gave a slight nod. They were a cool blue, identical to Walter's.

"Selected extracts, of course," said Director Granger.

He's giving me ten minutes to look through my file. Her heart bounced against her ribcage.

"I owe you a debt for helping my father." He frowned. "But after today, that debt is repaid. Canceled. Don't take advantage."

She nodded, not trusting her voice.

"Remember, your loyalties lie with C2. Don't reveal anything that you shouldn't. And remember that life will go on after tomorrow. For everyone involved. Think about what you want to do and say. Be careful."

Granger closed the door firmly behind him.

She stood, stepped toward the desk. Tentatively, she pressed one hand, palm down, on the folder, directly on top of the words *Jesse Sharpe*. Suddenly, unexpectedly, she was nervous. She knew what was inside that file. *Who* was inside it. Jesse smiled. *My family.*

Hello,

I've sneaked out from C2 for a little while and my friend, Christine Harris, has now set up an e-mail address for me:

jesse@christineharris.com

You could also use the Web site link www.christineharris.com/spygirl.html

Any secret communications should be safe. I hope lots of readers will write to me after they read my books. You can also use the Web site link to find puzzles, competitions, and a secret agent ID card.

— Jesse Sharpe,
child prodigy and hamburger lover

About the Author

Christine Harris is one of Australia's busiest and most popular children's authors. She has written more than thirty books as well as plays, articles, poetry, and short stories, and her work has been published all over the world. Her favorite colors are hot pink and purple.

GIRLS YOU'LL NEVER FORGET

A Corner of the Universe
by Ann M. Martin

In her twelfth summer, Hattie's small-town life is shaken by the arrival of her uncle. Hattie quickly bonds with Uncle Adam but fails to grasp the depth of his illness in this graceful, bittersweet exploration of friendship and loss.

Esperanza Rising
by Pam Muñoz Ryan

In this poignant story of hope in the face of hardship, Esperanza is forced to leave her life of privilege in Mexico, migrate with her mother to California, and work in fruit-picking labor camps during the Depression.

Missing May
by Cynthia Rylant

Summer is devastated when her beloved Aunt May dies suddenly. So is her uncle, until he believes his wife is contacting them from the spirit world. This Newbery Medal winner beautifully chronicles their journey through grief and love.

Available wherever you buy books.

www.scholastic.com

ON THE RUN

TWO FUGITIVE KIDS.
ONE BIG MISSION. THE CHASE IS ON!

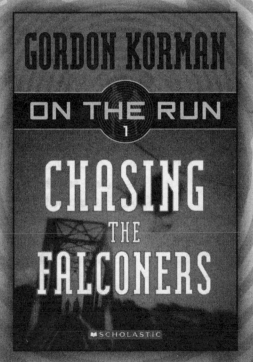

The Falconers are facing life in prison—unless their children, Aiden and Meg, can follow a trail of clues to prove their parents' innocence. Aiden and Meg are on the run, and they must use their wits to make it across the country, facing plenty of risks along the way!

SCHOLASTIC

OTRT